Morven *and the* Horse Clan

Luanne Armstrong

Great Plains Teen Fiction
(An imprint of Great Plains Publications)
233 Garfield Street South
Winnipeg, MB R3G 2M1
www.greatplains.mb.ca

SECOND PRINTING

Great Plains Publications gratefully acknowledges the financial support provided for its publishing program by the Government of Canada through the Canada Book Fund; the Canada Council for the Arts; the Province of Manitoba through the Book Publishing Tax Credit and the Book Publisher Marketing Assistance Program; and the Manitoba Arts Council.

Design & Typography by Relish New Brand Experience
Printed in Canada by Friesens

Library and Archives Canada Cataloguing in Publication

Armstrong, Luanne, 1949-, author
Morven and the Horse Clan / Luanne Armstrong.

(Great Plains teen fiction)
Issued in print and electronic formats.

ISBN 978-1-926531-74-8 (pbk.).--ISBN 978-1-926531-75-5 (epub).--
ISBN 978-1-926531-76-2 (mobi)
I. Title. II. Series: Great Plains teen fiction

PS8551.R7638M67 2013 jC813'.54 C2013-902800-5
C2013-902801-3

ENVIRONMENTAL BENEFITS STATEMENT

Great Plains Publications saved the following resources by printing the pages of this book on chlorine free paper made with 100% post-consumer waste.

TREES	WATER	ENERGY	SOLID WASTE	GREENHOUSE GASES
3 FULLY GROWN	1,301 GALLONS	1 MILLION BTUs	87 POUNDS	240 POUNDS

Environmental impact estimates were made using the Environmental Paper Network Paper Calculator 3.2. For more information visit www.papercalculator.org.

Dedicated with much love to my sister, Robin, and her horses.

Prologue

3500 BC

I was still a young girl when our land began to change. The expected rains didn't come. The first year was a spring and summer with no rain, then the next year we had a rainy season with not enough rain. Then yet another year with no rain meant the land began to dry to dust. The elders shook their heads. Through the length and breadth of our territory, it was the same. The women complained about not finding enough food: the berries dried on the stems, the seeds were scarce, the roots small. At night, children cried from hunger. I cried as well but my mother worked long and hard and managed to find enough plants and roots with which to feed me.

Over this time, with the continuing drought, the grass withered and the animals that fed on the grass disappeared. Thorny plants sprouted in place of the grass. Trees died, and in their place grew tangled brush with small thin leaves. The women wandered far, kept trying new plants; some were edible and some were not. The women would bring some spiny root or leaves home, cut them open, smell them, taste them, sometimes cook them, sometimes spit them out, shaking their heads. The men ranged far and wide in their hunting for game, and reported that it was dry wherever they looked.

Finally, when the rain failed again for a fourth year, there was a desperate clan meeting, and then another one, but no one knew what to do. The camp split along angry lines: those who wanted to stay and wait for the rain to return, and those who wanted to leave and look for a new, more welcoming territory. Both were risky; nothing was sure.

The split in the camp grew worse. The shaman came out of his tent and sat with the people who were most angry, listening to their complaints. The shaman was a wizened man named Luz who lived alone in his tent on the outside of the camp circle. His hair hung in two white braids down his back. He had a tangled wispy grey beard and very black eyes. Every day, someone took him food. Whenever there was a council circle, he came but usually said little.

One night, a woman who had two young children, a boy and a girl, and who had just watched one of her children die, ran screaming and tearing at her hair with her fingernails until the other women surrounded her. But she broke away from them, shouting at everyone: "We will die here. We will die. We must leave." The women tried to comfort her but she broke away from them and ran into the darkness.

The next day she and her family packed up and went away to the south. They looked back and then they looked forward and went over a rise and out of sight.

The rest of our people waited, sure the rains would come this year. The people watched billowing blue and purple clouds build on the horizon and then pass with only small drifts of rain. There was never enough to soak the ground. It was clear that it was time to go. But where? The scouts and hunters conferred but couldn't decide. Finally the shaman came out of his tent and silently pointed: north. The people packed their tents and what food they had, and set out.

And so our long journey began.

Chapter One

We came down the side of a rocky hill in a long straggling line. Brown spirals of dust marked our passage. We were all weary. Babies squalled. It had been a long walk today with little time to stop and rest. We needed water and food and the glint we had seen from the mountainside seemed to promise both.

I was near the back. I wasn't with the men or the women but in the space between. The women were ahead, the men behind. If I went with the women, where I belonged as a girl, my mother would find some work for me. If I went too close to the men, I would be sent away, and then the men would say something to my mother about it, and my mother would find reasons to keep me close to her.

So I slouched along, breathing dust. My bow was over my shoulder, unstrung. There had been little to hunt in these hills. The babies were crying and small children dragged their feet in the dust. But the men who scouted ahead had promised us water and now that we could see it, everyone began to move faster, the older children running ahead. The women hurried too, even burdened as they were with babies, hide bags, and bundled tents.

And now that we had found water, tomorrow the men would hunt—and so would I, but in a different direction from the men, and by myself.

It was almost dark by the time we reached the black pond. It had once been a small lake, but now a broad expanse of mud had dried around the edges, and dead reeds cracked in the chill evening wind. The water was set in a bowl of brown-gold hills, with animal trails winding down to the water's edge. The women trudged carefully through the mud to the edge of the water with clay bowls and waterhides; they began digging reeds in the darkness to get at the roots. Fires blossomed on the slanting lakeshore; smoke and the smell of food cooking soon filled the air. Gradually babies stopped crying and drifted to sleep, and the camp settled to darkness and an uneasy peace.

I helped my mother put up the tent, the two of us stumbling in the firelight, my two small sisters, Lailla and Deen, huddled beside the fire. "They could help," I snapped at my mother.

"They are too tired," she said gently. My mother's long black hair, usually so neatly braided, was coming loose and kept falling in her eyes. When the tent was up and staked into the hard packed ground, she and my sisters unrolled the bedrolls and the girls curled side by side to sleep. My mother and I sat by the fire. She brought out her finely carved wooden comb, sat behind me unbraided and combed out my long red hair, then braided it again. I relaxed against her knees. My mother almost never combed my hair. Usually she was impatient, nagging at me to help with the endless camp chores. It was such hard work to keep moving camp, to keep us all fed, to keep track of the many things we needed for our lives.

I wondered again why my hair colour was so different from everyone else's. I hated that it was red instead of black. This had made me feel from birth that I was an outsider; that I didn't belong to our people. Once, long ago at a clan Gathering, I had seen people with hair like mine. "Oh, they came from far away, from the north," my mother had told me. I wanted to ask her more questions but she held up her hand in warning and I had to be silent.

Now, after she finished with my hair, she sat staring into the fire. "Morven," she said finally, "tomorrow, you must hunt on behalf of your sisters. I know the men don't like you hunting. They will share what they catch with us, but your little sisters are growing weaker. We must have as much meat and fat as we can. I will gather roots and reeds tomorrow. We can rest here beside the water and gather our strength, but we won't be able to stay here long. The land around us is still too dry."

I sat silent. My mother rarely encouraged or even spoke of my hunting so I was glad for her approval.

"I don't understand why our land, that was once our mother and father and fed us all, has turned against us," she said. "Somewhere there is hope. Somewhere there is a green land. There must be or we will all die." I wanted to say something reassuring, but what?

"I must sleep and you must as well, my daughter," she said. She rose and went into the tent but I went on sitting by the fire, making plans for tomorrow, until my head drooped onto my knees.

In the morning, the camp was quiet. Most of the women and children were still sleeping but I knew the men would already have left to hunt. I folded the thin hide robe that I slept under and stowed it in a corner, slid my unstrung bow and a leather bag of arrows over my shoulder and slipped out. The sun wasn't up yet but I was eager to look around. This place was new to me, as we had been travelling hard and fast, looking for water. Now that we had found some, we could stay for a while and I could begin to learn this land. This water was a good sign. Perhaps there would be more water as we went further north; perhaps we once again would live in a place with animals and food in abundance. For now, I was just glad to be in a new place, with new territory to explore.

I trotted up the hillside into the warm light of the dawning sun. I paused when I reached the top of the first hill and looked down at the camp. The brown tents squatted like mushrooms in the dusty bowl of hills; the water glinted black, with gold and deep green at its center. I saw my mother come out, look around, and up at the hills. She knew I was there but she couldn't see me. She went to find dried grass and bits of wood for the fire and I turned my face towards the sun and began to move at a fast trot through brush and dry grass.

I was glad to be away from the camp and people. Our people had black hair and slanted, brown eyes, but my red hair and smoky grey-green eyes meant that people teased me, called me names: red crow, croaker, and worse. But my mother called me Morven.

From a very young age, I had preferred the company of animals to people. People made me uneasy. But I could sit for hours watching the patterns that ants made in their travels, or tracing the tracks of mice in the dust. I got so familiar with animals and became such a good tracker that some of our people thought I could talk to animals. And it was true, I often felt that animals spoke to me more clearly, in their own way, than the people I had known all my life.

My mother often told me a story of how I had always wanted to run away when I was a small child, how afraid she was of losing me. One day, I disappeared. She looked all day and finally found me playing with a family of dogs. The mother dog tried to bite her when my mother rushed in to grab me. I still liked the dogs that followed us from campsite to campsite. Most people ignored them. They ate scraps of hide and bones and guts and hunted for themselves.

Whenever I got the chance, I liked to sit and watch the life around me. I watched birds and small bugs and spiders and the busy lives of four-legged creatures. If I sat long enough, animals would lose their fear and forget I was there.

Now I sat quietly on the hill, listening and watching. The hot wind lifted my hair. Vultures wheeled on the wind.

Finally, I stood up and began to walk. All day, I trudged up dusty hillsides and looked out over a brown, empty land. I watched for tracks, for birds, I listened to the wind and noticed the dry, bitter smell of the grey plants that grew all over the hills. I stayed away all day.

That night, at dusk, when I stepped into the circle of made by the firelight beside my mother's tent, she said without looking at me, "Morven, the men say the land is still dry everywhere around us. What are we to do?"

"I know," I said. "I saw." I folded my legs and flopped down close to the fire. The evening was chilly.

"We will have to stay here, by the water and wait," she said. "The water here will sustain us for a while. If the rains come and the hills are green, we could stay in this place. If not, then we will have to move again. For now, there are roots, frogs, snakes, and bugs in the reeds."

I had come from my own hunt with little to show for it but I had heard and caught glimpses of small squeaking creatures, ones that I didn't know the names of, in the rocks. "Tomorrow I will set some snares," I said. My mother nodded.

But also, during my wandering, at the height of the sun, sitting on the highest hill I could find, I had seen faint dust spirals moving, thin lazy smoke against the sky. Tomorrow, I would go in that direction. Dust spirals meant something larger, meant a herd of some kind of four-legged beasts, and that meant food and now that I had some sense of the land, I could take time to go look at what had made the dust. Likely, the men would have seen them as well and would already be preparing for a hunt.

The next morning, I got up even earlier, and headed at a trot up the hill from the camp and went in the direction where I had seen the dust. I soon picked up the trail. I could tell from their round hoof prints that these were animals I had only seen a few times before, called horses. They had long ears, long hair on their necks, and thick black tails. Although I tested the wind and circled so they couldn't smell me, they sensed my presence and ran. I followed, long enough to tell they were going in a circle and coming back to where I had first surprised them. I came over a hill and saw them below me, their coats dark with sweat. I left them alone. They had done enough running. But this was exciting news I could bring back to the camp even if I had nothing to bring for food.

That evening, when I stepped into the firelight, my mother looked at my empty hands and sighed. She dipped me a clay bowl of food from the bowl set near the fire. Then she sat beside me, while both my small sisters crowded onto her lap.

"I saw dust trails," I said. "I tracked them. Horses. Lots of food if we can catch them. They ran away fast but they circled and came back towards here."

After I ate, I wandered to the edge of the camp. I heard a very faint snort. When I looked up, I could just barely see the horses, black dots on the high hilltop, watching us. I watched them until it was too dark to see. I wondered why they would come so close to humans. Then it hit me. Of course. We had driven them away when we came to the water. That is why they had circled around and why they were now on the hill above our camp. They needed the water just as we did, and they also wanted the grass that grew around the water.

The next morning, they were still there. Now I looked more closely and could see from the trails they were used to coming here for the water. Now we had taken it from them. Before we came here, it was their place.

The men had seen them too and had gone to their tents to get bows, arrows, and knives. They sat outside their tents, checking their arrowheads, sharpening their bone spearheads and arrowheads on smooth rocks, or making new arrowheads by chipping flint stones into sharp edges.

We needed food, and the horses would provide much more than roots and berries and the seed heads of grass, pounded and baked on hot rocks. The men gathered in a circle to plan the hunt and I sat on the ground, just outside the circle, listening. Horses were not easily caught. A hunt like this needed planning. Some glanced at me and most ignored me. My uncle Nazar, my mother's brother, looked at me and nodded. He knew that I was listening in order to learn more about hunting.

It is the men's job to hunt. Women hunt as well for small animals. But they are usually too busy to go on the longer hunting journeys that men take. My mother had patiently tried to teach me that women and men are different and do different things. She had tried to teach me women's skills: tanning hides, sewing clothes, cooking, looking after children. I hated it. Mostly I hated sitting in the circle of other women, listening to them chatter. I hated the way they looked at my hair, and I hated the way they laughed at my clumsiness and my bad sewing.

When I was very young, my mother found me crying in the tent after trying to sew. The other girls had laughed and called me names. She gathered me in her arms and rocked me. "Everyone has a place in our clan. Everyone has a something they bring to the people. You will find your place, little one. The people will no longer tease you but will look up to you."

But I still didn't know my place. I felt awkward around both the women and the men. So even though these are my people, my clan, my family, I went my own way most of the time and my mother looked at me and shook her head.

Our people didn't have to be very old before learning about the importance of food and the necessity of always ensuring that there was a supply of food nearby. Both men and women learned it as small children. But life got easier for the boys when they learned how to hunt. Then their bellies started to fill out and they swaggered around acting superior to the women and girls pounding seeds on the rocks. When I was very young, I couldn't understand why I couldn't learn to hunt as well.

I followed the older boys to learn how to set traps and snares. I tried to make myself a bow. My mother's brother, Nazar, found me one day trying to shoot my misshapen arrows with my badly made small bow.

"Come," he said. I followed him to his tent. He made me hold out my arms, felt them for strength, then measured a piece of wood against my height. A few days later, he came to my mother's tent with a strong bow and a full quiver of arrows.

My mother thanked him but said, "She needs to go with me to gather berries, not run after the men."

"Be patient, Botan. She can learn both ways. If she is gifted as a hunter, perhaps that is a good thing."

After this, from time to time, Nazar would take me with him hunting. He taught me much. But most of my hunting and tracking skills I learned on my own and from watching animals and how they behaved.

The next day the men killed a couple of the younger horses with arrows, and the rest ran. But that night, they came back and watched again from a distance. That night the camp feasted and people slept late the next morning.

At dawn, I went carefully up the hill and squatted where they couldn't see or smell me, and I could watch them. They were gaunt and hungry and their ribs stuck out like the ribs on our woven reed baskets. They needed food and water. Such skinny starved animals made poor food, but grass still grew tall all around the edge of the water where we were camped. That night, we feasted again on the meat from the two horses but with so many people, it was soon gone. The men would have to hunt again.

I lay awake for a long time that night, thinking. The next morning, again at dawn, I picked up one of my mother's woven reed baskets. It took only a short time to cut enough of the tall grass fill a basket. I carried it to the top of the hill. The horses scattered, fleeing before me as they would a wild cat.

I laughed. "I'm not your enemy," I called after them. Which wasn't true because I had eaten their flesh along with everyone else and would again. But I left the grass there.

They must have come back at night, for I never saw them, but the next morning the grass was gone. That day the men hunted again and I thought perhaps the horses would stay away. But the day after the hunt, at dawn, the horses came back, desperate for water.

This time, when I climbed the hill with a basket of grass, they ran from me again but not as far. They watched from a distance as I scattered the grass and went back for another load. I had soaked the second load of grass in water before I carried it up. This time when I came puffing and panting up the hill, they waited, not so far away, watching and snorting and talking to themselves. I wasn't fooled. It was the grass they wanted, and if they had to get my company along with it they would tolerate me.

I went away and sat down. I had found a hidden shady cleft in the rocks. I knew, today, the men had gone after different game that was slower and easier to catch; they had found an almost dried pond full of dying fish. So I spent all that day, undisturbed, watching how the horses were with one another. They fascinated me, something about the way they moved, something about how they were with each, polite, graceful, playful. These were different from the horses I had seen in the south. They were bigger, their legs were longer and their hides were brown or black or grey. Despite their boniness, their hides shone in the sun. Their eyes were huge and brown, always looking. Their black-tipped ears shifted constantly, listening.

The next time I came with a basket of grass, I kept my head down and my eyes and my body turned away as I'd noticed the young horses doing with the older leaders. This time, they only scattered a little. I spread out the grass, then made another trip and brought water in two waterskins. I emptied it into small hollows in the rocks. This time, they crowded around me, desperate for the water.

After a few more days, they let me walk in with the grass and water and dump it under their noses. Some of them reached out to smell me and blew air down their noses and then shook their heads at me. I imitated what they did. I blew air back and then bent my head away. We curved our bodies away from each other and some of the younger ones snorted and ran with their tails in the air to show their pride, and then snuck back to the grass.

It took me all the long hours between the high sun and the low sun to fill them up. By now they came crowding towards me and put their heads up and blew at me when I was coming. Their bodies no longer curved away from me. But still I kept my head down and acted with respect and good manners.

They had one need even greater than food, and that was water. Up above us, on the hills, the sun had burnt everything bare and dry, had taken away the little puddles and tiny crystal streams on which all the animals depended. We would have been starving ourselves if it weren't for the fact that the men had dug pits by the water and the animals coming down for water fell into them.

The horses came down as well, and several more were caught and killed. Some nights they scattered without getting any water, and the next day, they stood on the hills and watched us.

I felt sorry for them. Something about them pulled me. They bent their heads to sniff my hands. They were careful with me. They could have easily killed me. Instead, they were scared, but also, trusting. They were no longer just wild animals but animals I knew, like the dogs. Why was I working so hard to feed and care for them? I wasn't sure anymore.

But for now, I needed to find more water, otherwise the men would soon trap and kill all the horses. If I could get them away from the camp, they wouldn't be so easily trapped. When they ran away, the men couldn't hunt them because they were too fast. But the water held them. The waterskins were heavy and held too little. Besides, people were beginning to talk about this new foolishness and shake their heads. My mother frowned and shook her head when she saw me trudge by. They didn't understand what I was doing or why.

But when I wasn't carrying food to the horses, I spent my time alone in the hills, and I learned by watching and smelling and listening about the life that went on in the land around us, when no one was there to disturb it.

If there was this small lake, I thought, there must be other lakes, far over the hills, which wouldn't have us crouching beside them.

I went to look. It took me a whole day and all my skill to find it. While I walked, I watched the birds, the plants, where things grew. I knelt, dug at the soil, smelled the plants and looked at the shape of rocks. The country I walked through was seared and yellow, burnt by a sun grown too hot, nothing to eat, full of black rocks and steep cliffs. I could see where water had previously run down the cliffs, flooded ravines, and rolled rocks.

When I found the water, it was a small black pool hidden deep within a narrow rocky cleft. Red steep cliffs surrounded it. There were signs that other animals had come there, but not many, and no sign of other human clans having come there. All I had to do was persuade the horses to leave where they were and follow me and they would be safe. First I tried filling baskets with grass and carrying them, leaving a trail of grass to get their interest and going in front of the horses so they would follow. They did, for a while, but only for a while. Then the familiar territory called them back and one by one they left me there.

Then I thought perhaps if I acted as their enemy and got behind and pushed them somehow, they would go away and find the black water, but though I ran and shouted, they were too used to me by now and only ran a little way and then circled around me and came back.

I lay on the dry sand, panting from running and the heat, when a young male with shiny black hair came over to me. I had noticed him before. He was often at a distance from the other horses. I carried grass and water and put it in a special pile for him but the older mares usually drove him away. I often wondered why he was so alone. Now, he came up behind me. I lay very still. He put his head down, sniffed my hair and face. I put my hand up and he sniffed that as well, then walked away.

I rolled over, stood up and followed him. He turned. We sniffed noses and curved our necks and blew soft air at each other. I scratched gently along his back and he leaned against me.

After that, he often came to meet me and we played. One day I rubbed my hair against his; his hair was black and tangled. He was itchy and rubbed back against me then turned away and kicked his legs in the air, just missing me. I knew he had meant to miss and I laughed. I ran at him and turned and jumped, and he ran after me and then away.

After that I watched how the younger ones played and I played with them as well, but carefully, for they were much bigger than me, and so much faster, but I could roll and duck and hide more easily than them. After play, we would stand in a circle, our heads close together, puffing and blowing warm air, and then they would go back to eating and I would go back to my endless cutting and carrying of grass. While I worked, I tried to work through a tangle of emotions. The horses were no longer food; they were my friends. Each seemed like a character to me. And yet my family, my clan needed food.

An idea came to me one day while I was taking a rest from grass cutting. I was resting because I was tired and also because I was thinking about a new thing.

There was a girl named Lani whose tent was always across the clan circle from ours. The other children in our camp usually formed small packs and ran around together. But I had always been careful to go my way alone. Still Lani had always smiled at me, and sometimes, I stopped to talk to her before running off. One day when the older girls were teasing me, she said to them, "Stop. Morven is part of our clan too. You are being too cruel." The girls went away, embarrassed.

But today her hair looked like that of the horses; it was long and curly and shone in the sun. That hair pulled me. It pulled me across the circle and past the clan fire where the old men and women sat dozing in the hot sun. It pulled me like something shouting at me, come here, come here, and so I came. I sat down beside Lani. I had never really talked for long with her despite her friendly smiles. She was always doing something busy and important, scraping a small animal hide—the kind of tedious smelly work my mother was always trying to get me to do.

Now I sat there and said nothing. I had easily learned the language and the play of the horses, but I couldn't even talk to a girl my own age. She looked at me and smiled but just kept working. Finally, I left.

The next day, I sat beside her again. I picked up part of the hide she'd been working on and a bone scraper that was lying in the dust and we worked side by side for a while. I was awkward with the scraper and she giggled. Her giggle sounded like water flowing over round stones and for some reason, it went right through me the way I imagined a knife would.

"People say you are not really one of us any more," she murmured. "People say you are becoming a member of another clan, that soon you will leave us and take one of them for your mate."

I blew air softly down my nose like one of the horses would. Then I murmured back, "People of this clan are very foolish and often say what isn't true or shouldn't be said."

"It is true though," she went on, still laughing, "that you spend more time in the service of others not of your clan, and that when your mother or the elder women call you to pound seeds or scrape hides, you are usually not around."

"There are many to dig roots and pound seeds and scrape hides," I said. "That is not my work."

"Oh, and what is your work?"

I considered for a while. The scrapers went shh, shh, shh on the hide. The sun shone down as always and flies droned around our heads. The stink of the hide rose up around me. I had never noticed before how much hides stunk when they were ready to be scraped. "I am learning the language of the horse clan," I said. "It is a language of the body and not like the language which we speak at all. It feels like important work though I don't know why."

"Such work will not feed children," she said severely. "It is not work that keeps your people nourished. Why do you spend all your time at it? You could do both, you know. You could spend time scraping hides as well as that other foolish work." But she smiled when she said it.

After that, when I had finished carrying grass and water up the hill I went to sit with her in the drowsy heat of late afternoons. The food I supplied for the horses was better than nothing but it was never enough. It was exhausting work but at least the horses no longer came down the hill and into the traps set by the men. I had told my mother, knowing this information would soon spread through the camp, that I was trying to keep the horses healthy.

But they were getting thinner every day. Their coats no longer shone in the sun. They no longer played with me or with each other but crowded desperately around me when I came up the hill. Most of the younger horses had died and many of the older ones had fallen into the traps.

I was sitting with the Lani one day and watching the children play. Several of the smaller children were riding on the backs of the older children. They were having a mock fight, screaming and throwing sticks and lumps of mud. One very determined little girl had gotten hold of two hanks of hair and was yanking the head of the boy carrying her back and forth, in order to direct him. I watched this for a while and then I got up and went to my mother's tent. I sat down in the darkened tent and closed my eyes. An image formed in my mind. Yes, it was possible. It must be.

There was a pile of grass ropes curled in the back, used for wrapping the hides together when it was time to move camp. I took one rope and climbed back up the hill. By now, the horses crowded around to see what I had brought but since I had no food, they turned away.

I followed the young male that was my special friend. He was used to my touch. I showed him the grass rope, rubbed it on my hair and then laid it casually over his neck. I followed him all afternoon, and by the end of the afternoon, when I put gentle pressure on the rope, he moved in response to the pressure. I went down the hill with my head buzzing with excitement.

I went to find Lani but she was annoyed that I had left her so abruptly and wouldn't talk to me. I went to find food at my mother's fire but there was very little. "Oh, are you still one of us?" my mother asked furiously. "The water is empty of fish and even the animals come less often into the traps. The sun is eating up the land and soon it will eat us up too. You don't care. You've been too busy playing with your new friends, keeping them away from us. Do you think no one has noticed?" She turned her back to me.

I barely slept. I got up early to cut grass but there wasn't much of that left either. I had to persuade my friends to move, and soon. I spent the day with the black horse and the rope, only now I pulled and pushed in earnest. Soon he would go wherever I wanted him to go, although he let me know when he got bored and irritated with this new game. I wanted him to go to a new place.

I knew the men were angry. They had been watching me. They wanted to eat the rest of the horses and so they had decided to bait their traps with grass and water. From what I knew, they thought maybe I should be included in the hunt as well. Lani told me this. She was talking to me again. I kept bringing her presents. I brought her a red feather and a blue stone and a clear crystal I had chipped out of the rocks. She told me the men had warned my mother to keep me away from the horses.

The hunt would begin very soon, so Lani had told me. That evening, I went up the hill and slid the rope onto the neck of the young male. I walked ahead of my friend, pulling him on the rope. Sometimes he stopped and I had to pull him behind me like a sack of hides. But he followed. And the others followed him.

Soon we were out of sight of the camp and still they followed. I talked to them in whatever way I could, telling them of the black water and the green grass and moss around it and the absence of human hunters. They drifted behind me like smoke, but eventually, we were close enough to the new place for them to smell the water and then they began to snort and put their ears forward and shake their hairy heads at each other.

After a while they broke into a trot and then began to run. The young male ran with them and I let go of the rope and followed in their dust. They slid down the steep hill, and clambered over the black rocks to the new place, crowded around the water and drank deeply. The place was so steep they could only go one or two at a time, but they took turns.

When they had drunk their fill, they came back up the hill and stood beside me. But the ground around us was burnt dry and there was nothing for them to eat. The young ones nipped and kicked at each other in irritation. I lay on the ground and wondered what to do next. I wondered how long it would be before the hunters followed us. Would they kill me as well as the horses? Perhaps I shouldn't return to the camp at all.

I was exhausted and I slept for a while and when I woke, they were all standing around me, some sleeping while standing. My friend was standing beside me with his heavy head drooping. When I woke, I stood with him and he licked my hair and my hands. I rubbed my head and hands against him. We played together for a while and then we all wandered together while they searched for small shrubs and bits of grass to eat. No one came after us that day. Together we roamed around the rocky basin with the black-mirrored water at its deep center. I followed them all day, and this time when I walked beside the young male, I leaned on his back. By the end of the day I leaned my whole weight on him and let him carry me for the space of two breaths. He looked at me curiously. He didn't seem to care what I did. I thought that our relationship had changed. He was like a child. If I said, "Go there," he did and if I said, "Come here," he did.

The next day one of the older females smelled or heard something. She snorted nervously and tested the wind with her nose. I thought it must be the hunters coming, but the hillsides above us remained empty. All day the whole horse clan was uneasy. By evening, black clouds had begun to build in the southern sky. After months of clear sky, the sight of these clouds was strange. Lightning lanced down. A warm wind came and lifted the hair off my neck. The clan circled, uneasy. Plainly, they wanted to go somewhere else for shelter. Finally, one of the older mares moved off and the others followed. I followed as well, hanging onto the hair of the young male, but they went faster and faster and I couldn't see in the growing dark. I stumbled, almost fell, and he tried to pull away from me.

In desperation, I swung my leg over his back and sat where I had never sat before. I hung on with my legs and hands, my bum slipping and sliding at first. Then his speed smoothed out the bumps and we floated over the ground like an arrow flying. I balanced on his back, terrified at the speed we were going, faster than I had ever imagined anything could go. I clung to his neck while my hair whipped into my eyes and mouth. I opened my mouth and let the wind blow through me. I yelled in a combination of joy and terror. After a while, I sat up. I suddenly realized that sitting on his back was a lot like dancing, that I could balance there and let me body move with his. I was dancing with the thunder, dancing with the clouds, the lightning. I spread my arms, clung with my legs. I was flying with the wind.

The thunder of the horses' feet mingled with the thunder from the clouds that were chasing us and had by now, filled the sky.

A bolt sizzled down beside us and we went even faster, pitching and tossing in the blackness. Suddenly, I felt us sliding down a hill. I leaned forward, wrapped my arms hard around his neck and hung on. At the bottom, he stopped abruptly and I found myself sitting on his neck. I slid back and tried to see where we were. Warmth came up from his body like steam in the sweat tent. I had my hands wrapped in the hair on his neck. I still had my rope, tied around my waist and I leaned forward and tied it around his neck.

The storm broke around us. We all crowded together. My friend shook all over. I felt his fear come into me so I sat very still to show him not to be afraid. He shook every time the thunder cracked, but there was nowhere to go. I stayed on his back. After a while the storm moved away to the north and the rain came and soaked all of us. I slipped off his back and crouched under his belly, although it was a miserable excuse for a shelter. I was cold, tired and hungry. The insides of my legs were chafed raw. But my heart sang and thumped in my chest.

Something new had come into the world that I didn't understand when I slid on the back of the black horse. I could hardly wait to try it again. I dozed a little, crouched there. In the morning, when the sun came and warmed us both, he was still standing over me, even though his clan had moved off a ways.

I knew then that he had changed and our relationship had changed. He had given something over to me. I wasn't sure it was something I wanted, but it was something I had and therefore I had to take care of it.

I slid onto his back and together we went to the top of a high hill. I wasn't surprised to see our camp below. I urged the black horse toward my people's tents, and the other horses slowly followed. Then we all stopped.

Uncertain, I looked down at the tents. What would they say? Would my mother still be furious, or would she be proud?

I urged the black horse to go forward. He didn't want to; he danced around and jumped. I almost fell off and when we neared to the edge of the tents, the black horse stopped again, terrified. He danced around and threw his head back to show me his fear of going into the camp of his enemies.

We argued for a while and then he gave in and went the rest of the way down the hill and into the ring of tents. The people watched us. No one said a word. We went in and around the tents and stopped in front of Lani. Our eyes met. The men had followed and were standing just behind me.

I turned the black horse to face them. I was now taller than them, and faster. I took a deep breath.

"This is my friend and my partner," I said. "His family, his clan, are also my friends and partners. I declare them now and forever friends and partners of this clan and our people." No one said anything. No one interrupted me or teased me. Instead they all stared at me. They listened. Excitement and exhaustion gave me a new sense of boldness. I no longer really cared what they thought. "They will not be hunted anymore. Now that the rain has come, the hills will turn green again. We can travel and hunt. We will no longer have to hide here like animals in our own trap."

Suddenly one of the men stepped forward and yelled something I didn't catch. The black horse suddenly took off again, ran through the middle of the cluster of men who had to throw themselves out of the way.

He galloped right through the camp and had started up the hill before I finally stopped him and turned around. I wasn't really sure how I was doing any of this. I sort of thought about where I wanted us to go and somehow pushed and pulled on the rope and squeezed my legs to get us both to go in that direction.

But he had had enough. He wanted to be back with his herd. He put his head down and kicked up his heels. I flew over his head and landed on the ground.

When I opened my eyes, Lani was looking down at me. "Well, that was amazing," she said and laughed. "No one has ever seen such a thing. The men are all talking about your bravery, and wondering if you have been possessed by an evil spirit. The women are all talking about your boldness."

I groaned and sat up. Everything hurt but at least it all worked, more or less. The black horse was also standing just up the hill. The rope around his neck had tangled in a bush and stopped him. He was winding the rope around the bush, snorting and looking scared. I ran to him, unwound the rope, soothed him with my hands, and rubbed his head against mine. We leaned against each other and blew air together and I apologized.

Lani came and stood near us. He threw his head back and snorted at her and I showed her how to talk back, how to say hello and be polite.

"Does he have a name?" she asked.

I looked at him. "His name," I said, too grandly, "is Black Horse that Dances with Lightning." Then I lifted the grass rope off his neck.

He ran, kicking and bucking, back up the hill to be with his family. Lani stared at him and then at me. I could see so many questions and ideas dancing in her eyes but I was too tired to talk to her or anyone else. I walked back to my mother's tent, where I eased myself down beside the fire and my mother, for once, brought me food without complaining of my lazy ways. In fact, she didn't say anything at all. Her silence was ominous. I knew that quite soon I would have to explain what I had done. To her, and to everyone else.

Chapter Two

My life had changed. I had changed it. I had a friend in Lani and a friend in Black Horse. The men kept their distance. A furious discussion had broken out in the camp about the horses and what to do with me. I went to visit the horses every day and the rest of the time, I either sat in camp with Lani or wandered the hill.

The morning after I had ridden the black horse into camp, I was sitting by the fire, and my uncle Nazar sat beside me and asked me to tell him the whole story. When I was done, he shook his head. "This is a new thing," he said. "Who knows what it means or where it will lead? You are brave, Morven. Brave and crazy. What are we going to do with you? Morven, I am proud of you," he added. "I believe that you have made a change in the world but I am not sure yet how to think about it. The men have decided they will not hunt the horses. For now, anyway."

I knew the rain meant there would be other animals to hunt and trap, but it was something.

My mother brought us both food. "I am proud as well," she said quietly and smiled at me.

I was startled. She was proud?

But from the conversation I overheard between the men, the horses were still only food. My announcement about horses as our friends had turned into a joke to them. How could animals be our friends? When they saw me, they turned away, said things I couldn't hear to each other, and laughed.

One morning, Lani came up the hill with me and I introduced her to the rest of the horses. They were shy with her, they shook their heavy heads and snorted and the younger ones put their tails in the air and were silly. We spent the day moving slowly together and by the afternoon, a young female was spending more and more time beside Lani.

It took us several more days to persuade the female to accept the rope and then to let Lani slide on her back. I got on the black horse and we rode together. By the time we had accomplished all this, our legs were sore and our hands rubbed raw from the ropes. We went back down to the camp and then ran in the water. We splashed each other until we were cool and then we sat in the shade of the tent.

"We are using up the food around this place," she said. "Now the men are restless want to move. They want to go hunting. They say the land will soon be dry again. The women say they are not ready," she added, She was pounding seeds. Lani was always working. So I helped as well, although often I simply sat and watched Lani at her work.

This was often the case, that the men wanted one thing and the women another. Usually it got talked over and over and chewed up and spat out long enough that everyone got tired of arguing and a decision was made without anyone really making it. I was ready to move myself but I hadn't thought about the horses. The adventure of getting to know them had been enough to preoccupy me.

"I don't think the horses will come with us," I said. They won't leave this place that is their home."

I began rolling grass in my hands, then twining it into strands that would then become a rope. This was one of the few camp chores I was good at. It made my mother happy when she saw me making rope. At least it was something useful. Ropes were everywhere but they didn't last very long. Ropes were made of grass, or bark, or leather. But there was always a need for more.

"What if we tried to make them come with us?" Lani asked.

I pointed with the end of the rope at one of the dogs snuffling around the fire pit. Some people threw rocks at them but they never seemed discouraged. There were always enough scraps around to keep them hopeful. I liked them. "You mean, like the dogs? They follow us for food."

Lani said. "And they're useful. They clean up the camp. They warn us. What can horses do?"

"I don't know. I just like them. I thought they were your friends too."

Lani sighed. "The children are still crying at night. There still isn't enough food. I agree with the men. We have to move. That's what is important."

"Maybe it will rain again."

"Maybe it will," said Lani. "But when?"

I sighed. Secretly I agreed with her. I was tired of squatting by this muddy puddle of water. I wanted to be moving. I wanted to be hunting. I wanted to be looking over a hill onto new land, full of possibility.

"There will be other horses," I said. "We saw them before. We can make friends again."

"The men want to kill these before we go. We can dry the meat and carry it with us. Now it will be easy for them."

I was silent. I knew she was right again about the men killing the horses and I knew there was nothing I could do about it. Despite my declaration of friendship between the horses and our people, the men were simply biding their time and then they would do what they had to do to keep the people fed.

I kept playing with the new rope, winding it around my arms and hands and then finally around my waist.

"I have to go," I said. I stood up and walked through the camp with my head down, conscious as always, of eyes on me, feeling them tearing at my skin with tiny hooks. I went up the hill but the horses were nowhere in sight. I went up to a knoll of black bumpy rock from where I could see the camp and well beyond, I saw a movement from the corner of my eye. It was one of the scavenger dogs from the camp, a young one with black and grey spots and yellow eyes. For some reason, he had followed me. He paused when I turned to watch him, as if ready to run, but when I stood still, he stood.

Dogs were like flies, or birds. Just around. I liked them. I gave them bits and scraps of food when I had it. Sometimes I sat with them or curled up in the dust beside them. They were interesting to watch.

But this dog was acting strange. I wondered if he wanted something or if he was sick. We watched each other for a bit. He had his head down, as if he were studying the ground in case something interesting might be happening there. But the tip of his tail was wagging in tiny circles. He reminded me of the way I looked when I wanted some food from my mother and she was mad at me. I laughed and he looked up, then backed away a few steps and sat down. I sat down as well. I put my head on my knees and ignored him. I thought he would leave when I didn't feed him. Instead he lay down.

Far away, below me, I could see the people in the camp, moving, busy, doing chores, talking to each other. Farther away, the edge of the land shaded into dark green and purple. The sky was a deep blue but small puffs of clouds left shadows on the grey dusty hills.

I kept half an eye on the dog. Whenever he thought I wasn't watching, he crept imperceptibly closer, crawling on his belly.

I had a bit of dried meat in a pouch at my waist and I pulled it out and put it on the palm of my hand. I put my head down again until I felt his nose on my hand and the meat disappeared. I took my hand back and pulled out a bit more. When the meat was gone, he waited expectantly to see if there would be more. I put my hand up. Usually, any dog would run at such a sign, sure there would be a stick or a rock coming at them. Instead, he looked at my hand, and then he sighed, flopped onto the ground, curled up with his nose on his front paws and was instantly asleep. Or so it appeared.

Suddenly, his eyes opened, his head came up. He sprang to his feet. He stared intently at something. I stared as well but I couldn't see anything. Then finally I spotted what he was watching, a ground squirrel on top of a rock. Once he had figured out what it was, he lay back down and went back to sleep. But I noticed that his ears twitched at every bird call. At my smallest movement, one eye would open then close again.

I was impressed. I was a good hunter, but he could see and hear things that I couldn't. "You are a good hunter," I said out loud. "You see and hear well." He looked at me and yawned. "Next time I go hunting, maybe you should come with me." He wagged his tail just a tiny bit, only the tip. "If you help me, you can share the food." His tail wagged again. He was young enough that he had probably only recently left his mother. When I stood up to go down to the camp, he followed. When I sat down next to Lani, he flopped down behind me.

She laughed. "Another friend?"

"Perhaps all the horses can come with us." I said. I had been thinking hard on the hill.

"You would have to make them," she said.

"I want them to come; they can be part of my clan."

Lani frowned. "No," she said. "It won't work. People are already very angry that you kept food from the people, that you give your loyalty to the horses. Morven, you can't belong to the horse clan and the human clan. You have to put your people first."

I sighed. "Maybe I will just stay here alone."

She put down her work and looked at me. "Oh, Morven," she said, "you are alone too much already. You walk alone, you sleep alone, and you hunt alone. But people are your family, not the horses. The people keep you fed and safe. Even when people are angry at you, no one refuses you food or greetings, no one shuns you. Do you want to break those ties?"

"They call me names. They laugh at me."

"But they care for you as well. Your mother, your uncle, they worry about you. "

I shook my head, ignoring her. Then I said, thinking out loud. "Or, I could go ahead of the people, like the men scouts do, but faster. When I find land where we all can live, I will come back for the horses. It is too dry for them here. I will make them come with me. I did it before, I can do it again."

She considered this and picked up her work again. The bone hide scraper went swish, swish over the wet and stinking hide.

"Morven, you are like a crow, trying to keep all of your sticks in one nest. You want the horses, you want your family, and now you want to be with us and not with us. Can such a thing be done?"

"I want what I want," I snapped.

"You are a foolish dreamer," she snapped back.

I couldn't speak. If I did, I would say something angry and I didn't want to lose Lani as a friend. Instead, I stood up and left. The spotted pup followed.

I sat beside my mother's fire that night poking at the flames and adjusting tiny bits and pieces of wood so they would burn without smoking. My mother was gone to the council and since I hadn't escaped soon enough, she had told me to stay and feed the children.

I had piled stones into the fire and when they were red hot, I lifted them out with tongs and put them into a basket of water with small bits of dried meat to which I had added powdered marsh roots. If I put hot stones in the water long enough, the water would cook the meat and roots and then we would all eat the meat and drink the juice.

My mother's other little girls were much younger than me. My mother also had several sisters and sometimes their children crowded into the tent at the smell of cooking food. It was one reason I sometimes avoided my mother's tent; it was always too crowded. If I slept there, I often found one or two small children curled next to me in the morning. I tried to be nice to them, but I wasn't very interested in children. My sisters took all my mother's time and attention.

I remembered being with my mother before she had other children. She paid close attention to me then, despite my red hair. I would sit between her legs as she worked and talked with the other women. When she had to go somewhere, my mother would tie me to the tent with a rope to keep me from running away, because I wouldn't stay with the other women. I would sit on the ground and imitate the cries of the hawks and other birds circling overhead. If she left me alone, I would wander out of camp, following a bird or a mouse or a beetle.

I always knew I was different from the other children. As I got older, the bands of roving children in the camp began to follow me and call me names but I soon learned to avoid them and they never followed me far. After a while, I began to spend more and more time out of camp, coming in for food or sleep. My mother was always busy with work or a new child and she let me go easily enough. Nazar was kind to me, and our shaman, Luz would sometimes come and sit with my mother and me at our fire.

While I sat beside the fire, I began thinking. Perhaps I should just go away on my own. I was so tired of being stared at, of feeling alone. Perhaps the black horse and the spotted dog could be members of my new family. I would have to feed and care for them the way my mother fed and cared for all of us. I would get a hide and make my own tent. I would pack my things and then I would go ahead into the new land and then the camp would no longer laugh and jeer at me. I began thinking about what I would need.

This was a whole new idea, the idea of being alone. Even though I spent most of my time alone, the camp was always there, safe, full of food, noise, warmth, and a place by my mother's fire to sleep. Could I hunt enough to feed the spotted pup and myself as well? He would help me hunt but then we would have to share our food. I would have to persuade the black horse to come with me, and then I would also have to ensure that he always had enough food and enough water.

The more I thought about it, the more frightening, overwhelming, and exciting it seemed to be. My head hurt. It was crowded with visions and thoughts, pictures, noise. It was too much. I put my hands over my ears, my head on my knees, hoping it would subside.

But the crying of the children brought me back to myself. I used a pair of sticks to pull a piece of meat out of the hot water, then stuck it in my mouth. Cooked enough, I thought. The minute the other children saw me eating, they scurried forward, sat around the woven reed container. I speared out bits of meat for each one with a stick, cooled it by blowing on it, and handed each a chunk. They stuffed it in their mouths and sat chewing with juice running down their chins, eating as fast as they could. I had to swat a couple of the older kids out of the way so that the smallest children could eat.

The food disappeared almost immediately. The children were still hungry. Their bellies stuck out. Their eyes were huge in their faces. We needed more food than this. Once we had bales of dried meat mixed with berries and fat, wrapped in hides and stored in the back of the tent. Once the women had more grass seed than we all could eat. Once we had strips of dried meat and fish on racks outside the tents.

If I were gone, there would be one less mouth to feed, one less for my mother to worry about.

"Go to bed now," I hissed at the children. They kept looking in the container as though it might magically hatch more food until they finally got discouraged and drifted away to their sleeping robes.

My mother stepped in the circle of firelight, flopped down beside me, stooped and weary.

"There is no more food," I said.

She shook her head. "Tomorrow the men will hunt your friends, we will dry the meat and carry water and then we must go. This place that was our refuge will quickly become a trap unless it rains again. But there is no sign of more rain coming."

We both stared into the fire. There was nothing more to discuss and we both knew it. My mother put her hand on my head and stroked my hair. I wondered if she knew what I was thinking and planning. I would have to sneak away from the camp or she would never let me go. Would she miss me? She was always so busy. Perhaps it would be easier for her if I were gone. Would Lani miss me? I would miss her but I didn't want to think about her.

Chapter Three

We needed water, all three of us, the spotted dog, the black horse, and me. The sun was our enemy. We travelled at night and slept in the shade during the day. At least the dog and I slept, while the black horse struggled to find food. He missed his family; I missed mine. But his family was dead and mine was behind us somewhere in the heat and the dust.

I had left the camp many days earlier, creeping quietly away in the dawn light. I had taken my bow, my sleeping robes, some full water skins and some food. People in the camp were sleeping.

I had been called to the men's circle the night before, and had sat in silence.

Lazar said, "Morven, the people must have food. The horses are your friends, yes, but the only way they can serve your people is for food. They are not our friends. I have listened to your story and I am proud of your bravery but I cannot let your mother and your sisters starve."

Then suddenly and abruptly, Luz spoke. "We don't know yet what she has done or what it means. Let her keep the black horse. Let her be who she is. Leave her be."

The men muttered but no one was willing to argue with Luz. "We will have enough food to travel," he said. "Somewhere there is a green land for us. I have seen this." And then he rose, and wrapping his robe around himself, went back to his tent.

I got to my feet and went back through the darkness to my mother's tent. My heart was bitter. That was the night I decided to leave. I didn't want to stay and watch Black Horse's family die. I didn't want to tell my mother or Lani. They would only argue with me. Instead, I got my things together and left.

The spotted dog had come with us and I was glad to have him. Anger at my people coupled with the thought of adventure had pulled me out of the camp. But now the waterskins were empty and so were our bellies and I was fast beginning to realize how foolish my adventure really was. All three of us watched, for food and for water. We were a good team. We had found small springs in a few places, enough to keep us going, not enough to let us stay.

Once, a spring seeped from the base of a cliff. Another time, when I had seen a clump of bush and trees growing in a gully, I had dug into the ground and found water. But now we had been three days without water and we were desperate. The spotted dog slouched along behind us panting, and the black horse lagged at the end of the rope I had tied around his neck.

Now I thought about my people, somewhere far behind me. I didn't know where they were, if they wondered where I had gone or whether they were following me. Although I was still angry, I missed them far more than I had expected.

After the first few days, a sense of terrifying loneliness seemed to bounce off the red barren rocky hills, the bright sand, the black rocks, and echo all around me. I decided that, once I found water I would go back, find them, and make out that this is what I had meant to do all along.

If they'd left the waterhole, they would be in bad shape by now. The children would be listless in the heat; the women would have to carry them along with the bundles of tents and sleeping robes and food.

It was still morning but the sun was already too hot to travel. Finally, we all stopped in the shadow of a tall cliff; there was a cleft there we could crowd into to hide from the sun. The spotted dog flopped and the black horse stood with his head down, eyes almost closed. I left them there and climbed the cliff above, the rocks burning my hands and feet. From far above, the sandy plain stretched out ahead of me, blue, misty, endless. It was mostly rocks and brown baked dirt, with small bits of brush dotted here and there.

I waited, patient and desperate. There had to be something, some sign. I refused to die, even if I had been foolish.

I pulled my sleeping robe over my head and dozed in its sparse shade. The spotted dog roused me. He was standing sniffing the air, looking out onto the plain. I followed his gaze and I saw them as well, a line of black dots crossing the expanse ahead, deer, maybe, or more horses. But where there were other animals, there was water. We had to find their tracks and follow them.

It took effort to get the black horse moving. Finally we crossed the line of tracks and turned to follow them. I could see bits of green, and as we got closer, the tops of trees. Finally, we got close enough to the trees, for us to smell water; the black horse perked his ears and then he was running and dragging me behind him.

The water was a green, scummed over pool about the size of two tent rings. Tall trees with shiny huge leaves grew around it. Not many, but still trees. The tree trunks were grey and cracked. Plumes of wiry, grey grass ringed the pool and brush grew out to the edges of this place, making it seem closed in. There were other small harmless animals there, ground squirrels and mice and even tiny fish in the water.

We drank and slept through the long hot afternoon. The black horse snatched hungrily at grass and leaves. I climbed the trees and ate some of the fruit that hung there; it was good though slightly green and bitter. I found some plants that were familiar and I built a small fire from twigs and grass and put in stones to heat so I could make tea.

There were reeds in the pool and I dug some of those and cleaned off the roots and put them in the fire to roast. It wasn't much but it was enough. The spotted dog nosed through the dried grass and found small creatures that squeaked and ran before he pounced and snapped them up.

It was amazing what a difference a bit of cool water and some small bits of food made to all of us. The spotted dog came back to where I was sitting by the small fire, lay down and began licking his paws. The black horse grazed nearby. I congratulated myself on finding this water and food. I played with the spotted dog's soft ears and he licked my hand. Black Horse came put his heavy head on my shoulder and we all dozed for a bit in peace.

But as the afternoon wore on and the red sun began to sink towards the dusty horizon, the atmosphere around the pool began to change. The spotted dog perked his ears and got to his feet, growling. The grove of trees had suddenly become very quiet.

I went quickly and softly to the side of the black horse. He had begun to blow air hard down his nose and swing his head, trying to smell and see something that was frightening him. He jumped away from me but I was too fast for him and slid onto his back. I had left the rope around his neck and now I gathered it up. I felt his muscles bunch and quiver between my legs. He was shaking, and he tossed his head and snorted, pawed the ground, jumped sideways, but still, he waited for me to decide what we should do and where we should run.

Then the black horse shifted under me and jumped again. Now he and the spotted dog were both pointing in the same direction, ears pricked. Suddenly the dog ran forward, barking and howling like a maniac. A huge cat, tawny, black stripes, with a long tail and enormous teeth stuck its head out of a patch of thick bush, and began to stalk forward, its tail twitching, its head down. This was too much for the black horse, who turned and bolted, taking me with him.

Behind me I could hear snarls and frantic barks, and then the spotted dog caught up with us even though the black horse had his head down and was running hard. It was all I could do to stay on his back; I held onto the rope around his neck and he ran and ran. I turned to look but the huge cat wasn't chasing us. Gradually, when I thought we were far enough away, I pulled back on the rope, cutting off his air. He slowed, and stumbled and then, finally, stopped.

He stood with his head down, puffing, his sides heaving. The spotted dog sprawled under his feet, panting. Blood was running from a cut in one shoulder but judging by how hard he had run he wasn't badly hurt. I slid off the black horse and fell on the ground, my legs shaking. I lay there for a while and then the spotted dog did a strange thing; he crawled over to me and licked my face. I put my hand on his head and he licked my hand. He whined and shook and the black horse stood over us both, still panting but breathing easier now. I realized that the two of them had probably saved my life, if only in trying to save their own. The spotted dog could have run away but he hadn't, he had stayed behind and stood up to the cat just long enough for me to get away. I patted him again and he sat up and leaned his weight against my shoulder, looking in the direction from which we had come, his nose wiggling, ears perked. I had thought I was their guardian but they were mine as well.

I looked around to see where we had stopped. I could see our tracks in the sand; they led back over a sand hill. Far in the distance were the treetops of the place where we had found refuge; I had filled bags with water and food. They were still back there, lying on the ground. My sleeping robe, my bone knife, my other ropes, my firepot, flint, all the supplies I needed, we all needed, to survive, were still back there. I would have to go back. But for now, I sat on the ground, shaking and seeing over and over, the huge striped gold and black head of the cat emerging from the bush, its lips wrinkled in a snarl over its curved teeth.

We spent the whole long night sitting and watching; every sound made me jump. Finally, I curled up on the sand and the spotted dog curled up against my belly. The black horse stood over us all. I dozed a bit. The sand was cold and hard and I missed my warm sleeping robe. I missed my bow, my cooking basket and my snares. I missed my mother and Lani. I even missed my squalling little sisters.

When the first light came, dull and grey, we started back. The black horse didn't want to go; he stopped and jumped sideways and snorted. But slowly, he came. As we neared the ring of trees, I saw a strange thing. Animals waited, just outside the trees. Tiny delicate deer, twitching their ears in terror, rabbits, foxes, all staring into the trees. It was a trap. They were as desperate for water and food as we were. Until one of them became thirsty and desperate enough to dash in, and provide the giant cat with breakfast, the rest would have to suffer. I waited with them; we all waited as the sun rose and the heat began to pound at us like a giant fist. The other animals got increasingly restless; small groups of them began to dash backwards and forwards, while the rest jumped around restlessly. Then suddenly they all broke at once, running madly towards the water. The big cat sprang instantly, grabbed one of the small deer, shook it and then dragged it away into the brush.

I could see the relief go through the other animals. They crowded around the water, drank and then trotted away. I pulled on the rope and dragged the black horse behind me to the water. He was nervous but he drank, as did the spotted dog and I.

Frantically, I grabbed my things, flung them into a bundle, and slung them over my back. I yanked the two water-filled skin sacks I had, tied them together and slung those over the other shoulder. Then I flung my leg up, got myself on the back of the black horse, and we left that death trap. The giant cat stuck his gleaming head with its yellow eyes, out of the bush and watched us go.

Chapter Four

Three days later, we struggled our way up another rocky dry hill, looked out and saw a haze of green in the valley before us. We came down the other side, and gradually, as we worked our way lower and lower, we saw clumps of grass, and then bushes and then small trees. The poor black horse, who hadn't eaten much of anything for three days, snatched at every blade of grass and leaf. But we couldn't stop until we found water. The skin bags were empty.

Suddenly the black horse threw up his head. His nostrils flared. The spotted dog did the same. They both charged forward, me with them, and as we all stumbled down the hill, I could finally hear it too, the wonderful blessed trill and trickle of water over stone, a sound I had almost forgotten. A small creek ran in the bottom of the valley; everything we needed was there, grass and water, and so there would be food as well, roots, plants, berries, animals, plus wood for a cooking fire.

I fell off the black horse and we all buried our faces in the water. I stuck my head under and let water wash the dust from my matted hair, face and ears. The water was cool and tasted like happiness.

That night I stared into the fire and tried to make a decision. Should I go back and find my people, tell them what I had found, a valley with good water, food, a land where we could survive, at least for while? Or should I keep looking? I didn't know if this land continued, if there were people already living here, or if there just would be more desert ahead.

And to find my people, my clan, would mean retracing my footsteps across the dry land, facing down the enormous cat again, dealing with heat and thirst again. I didn't know if they would be waiting for me. I had snuck away. Perhaps they thought I was dead.

But could I stay here by myself, with no family, no friends except for a horse and dog? I missed my mother. I missed Lani. I even missed Nazar and old Luz. But I didn't miss the men laughing together.

Finally, I decided to wait until the next day, when I had time to look around. I fell asleep sitting there, and then woke up and crawled into my robe and slept until the light woke me.

Neither the black horse or spotted dog were near me, but I could hear where they were. The black horse was beside the creek, tearing hungrily at the grass and leaves and the spotted dog was crashing through the brush along the creek, hunting. I knew I needed time to rest; I could feel tiredness in all my bones and muscles, but I also needed food.

I followed these sounds to where the spotted dog was hunting and found him lying on the ground, chewing the guts out of a rabbit. I came closer and he raised his head and growled. Fair enough, he had caught the food but I wanted a share. I had shared whatever I had with him. I bared my teeth and growled back. I snatched at the rabbit and instead of fighting, he backed away, still growling. I took the dead limp carcass back to the fire, dismembered it and threw the bones, skin and guts to the dog, who gulped them all down. After he was finished, he came to me, wriggling his body like a small child, and licked my hands.

I slept and woke and ate and drank and slept some more. On the morning of the third day, I woke and knew that the strength had come back into my arms and legs and I was myself again. But that meant the decision of what to do next still had to be made and I couldn't make it yet. Instead, I dug and cleaned roots; many of the plants here looked familiar. There were fish in the small stream and I wove a basket into a fish trap, and caught and split to dry as many fish as I could. I needed more water bags but without a deer hide or any hide from an animal larger than a rabbit, I couldn't make one. If I went back, perhaps I could leave the spotted dog and the black horse here to manage on their own until I came back. Until we all came back together...my mother, my uncle, the children, and of course, the men who would be jealous that I had found this place and not them.

In the late afternoon, I caught the black horse, climbed on his back and we all went exploring. We crossed the creek and climbed to the top of the hill on the other side. From the top of that low hill, I could see there were a few other low hills covered with grass, with trees in the hollows between the hills but beyond that a bare plain that was probably just more desert.

We came back down the hill and followed the creek upstream for a while. It wound and wandered its way among low hills. When I climbed to the top of one of these hills, all I could see in the distance was a haze and beyond that, more dry plain but with more grass than the land I had crossed after I left my people. So far as it went, this was good land. But it obviously didn't go very far. But here, perhaps, my people could find a new home for a while, or at least a place where the children would no longer cry at night with hunger.

So far I hadn't seen anything as large and terrifying as that tiger, but I thought there must be other predators around. There were lots of birds, rabbits, fish and deer, and that much game would attract predators.

The land seemed peaceful, but as I looked closely I began to notice human signs, places where the brush had been bent back, paths worn by use, and finally, stones that had been used to hold down a tent. People had been here, might still be here. I slid off the black horse and found a trail.

I began to follow the tracks, still going upstream. The signs of humans got more numerous and the spotted dog began to growl deep in his throat. My bare feet were silent on the dusty path. I turned and retreated back onto the horse, and then back to my camp.

I had never met new people on my own before. In my clan, we rarely saw other people. There were occasional Gatherings, when a lot of people came together but these were a lot of work and involved travelling long distances, so they didn't happen often. But whenever the shamans decided it was the right time, we all met at a Gathering somewhere. We stayed for many days, singing, dancing, eating a lot, visiting back and forth. I had been to several such Gatherings in my life, and I remembered them as times of noise and confusion—so many people around was hard for me to deal with—but also, I remembered the joy and delight on the faces of my clan as they danced, or told stories, or reconnected with old friends.

And whenever we encountered a new group of people in our travels, it was always—after some initial hesitation until we got to know each other—cause for a celebration, for dancing and singing and stories.

I slept uneasily that night, still troubled by not knowing what to do. I knew I didn't want to meet these strange people, not on my own. I thought I would get up early and leave before they discovered me.

The next morning, I rose as soon as the light turned grey. I rolled my sleeping robe, picked up my bow, my digging stick and slung the two full bags of water over my back. It was the spotted dog that alerted me, barking and growling. I turned to see where he was looking but I couldn't see anything through the trees. But after my experience with the giant cat, I didn't wait to see what was attacking us. I ran for the black horse, intending to jump on his back and get out of there, fast.

Then I heard voices calling, and two men came out of the brush. They stood still, waved to me, put their hands out, open, to indicate friendliness. One had a spear and another a long stick. They both had net bags slung over their shoulders and one had what looked like a small deer in the bag.

I stood still and then I turned and came back to the still-smoldering fire. The two men came slowly forward. I looked around but I couldn't see the black horse. He had run away. The spotted dog stood at my side and growled low in his throat.

The two men gabbled something at me and I stared. It was language but not my language. Then one of them moved his hands and I recognized some of the trade signs my people used when strangers came by. The other people that we knew and occasionally saw and traded with sometimes didn't talk like us but we all had a system of signs we could understand. The men were strange looking, small and dark. They both had long braided black hair and thin beards.

"How far have you come?" asked the man's hands.

"Far," I indicated, waving my own arms back in the direction of the desert.

"People?" he asked, and I shook my head, held my hands palm up to show I was alone and meaning no harm. The spotted dog was still growling, his ears flat and his tail stiff.

The first man glanced at the other man, who grunted and then pulled a small deer carcass out of his bag. He bent to the fire, piled some twigs and leaves on it and blew on it until there was flame. With a few deft swipes of his rock knife, he cut off a few strips of meat and strung them on a stick to cook.

When I squatted at the fire, the dog lay down beside me. He wrinkled his lips and showed his teeth at the men. One drew back his leg to kick at the dog and I held out my arm to protect it.

"No," I said. "He is my friend and protector." They couldn't understand the words but they looked at my outstretched arm and then at each other. The taller of the two shrugged. He looked at me and then at the dog. He squatted and put his hand out to the dog, who sniffed it. The man looked at me and smiled. I realized he was young, almost as young as me.

They were both same height as me. Their skin was darker than mine and their noses shorter and rounder than the long thin noses of my people. They both looked well fed.

We ate the meat together, then they stood up. They motioned for me to come with them.

"Wait," I said, holding up my hand. I picked up my rope and all my other gear and then went away through the brush. It took me a while to find the black horse and when I came back with him, they both jumped back, startled.

I had been gone long enough from my own clan to have forgotten how strange it might seem to them. They backed away as if I was leading a tiger.

"Horse," I said in my language, "friend," and then I made the sign for friend, for peace.

They looked at each other again. I turned and stroked the sleek shiny warm neck of the black horse, and then I slid onto his back. They stared, and I slid off again.

"Come," I said, beckoning. They came forward. The black horse poked out his nose and blew at them and they jumped back again. I laughed and they looked offended. I took one of their hands and held it out for the horse to smell. I blew in his nose and we rubbed out shaggy heads together the way we both liked to do. The men laughed and shrugged looking at each other and not at me.

They backed away, shaking their heads and muttering to each other in their own language. Then they turned and headed into the brush and I followed with the black horse and the spotted dog. I decided that it was necessary to see who else lived there, and most especially, to see that they were friendly, and then if my people came here, I would be able to show them it was safe. These two men seemed friendly and kind.

Their homes were cleverly hidden in a ravine, a cluster of huts made of wood, not hides, but there was a fire burning in the centre, women and children, and strange dogs huddled around the outside of the circle of huts. The spotted dog bristled and growled; the black horse threw up his head and stopped in his tracks. It was a job to persuade them both to come with me into the midst of the huts. When they did, they both crowded next to me, the dog so close to my legs that it was hard to walk, and the black horse with his head almost tucked under my arm.

As we came in, everyone stopped what they were doing and stared as if I was some strange monster, instead of just an ordinary looking redheaded girl. The men were talking and waving their arms around; they pointed at me and the horse and the dog. The other people let their mouths gape open. I stared at the ground. While I had been alone in the desert, I had forgotten how much I hated being in a crowd and being stared at. Perhaps I had made a mistake, I thought. Hunger and thirst were in some ways easier to cope with than this intense scrutiny. But I stood still and waited. Finally, a woman came forward. She looked a bit like my mother. I could tell the men were respectful of her. They backed off. There was some more talking and hand waving and the men turned away.

The woman looked at me. She had wary brown eyes but they weren't unfriendly. She made signs for food and water and I nodded. She led me forward to the fire where I collapsed cross-legged in the dust, still holding the rope that bound the black horse to me. She brought me water in a clay cup, and some bits of dried meat on a leaf. This is what my people do as well, on the rare occasions when a solitary visitor comes. Such visitors are important because they always bring news. They need to be fed and looked after and then listened to.

The woman sat beside me. She pointed behind me in the direction I had come and I nodded. She held up one finger and I nodded again and then I held up many fingers and pointed them in the direction I had come. Then I tried some of the language signs I knew for water and people. She knew some of them but many of her hand signs were different from mine. But we had a conversation, using signs and pointing, nodding, and generally waving our arms around. It mostly worked. There was a lot to explain…about the horses, the desert, and my family. I thought she understood. Some of the words in their language were similar to ours. We began to compare words and sounds and began to work out bits of a shared language.

After a while, the black horse, standing behind me, grew impatient and butted me hard with his head. The crowd of people that were still standing around us, staring and talking in their own language, found this very funny. Everyone laughed. I got to my feet and led him out of the camp. They all followed. Their camp was beside the creek and all three of us had a drink. They all watched. I took Black Horse up the hill to where there was grass and turned him loose to eat. They followed me.

Finally, I made my own fire, unrolled my sleeping robe, tied the black horse with a long rope so he could eat. They continued to watch as if every move I made was something strange. Only when I lay down, did they all go away and let me sleep.

In the morning, I lay, still half asleep, going over the past few days in my mind. I knew I had made a decision. I was going back, I was going to find my people again and lead them through the desert to this place where they could rest and recover. These people were friendly, they had food, perhaps they would take us in and help us get strong again, and then we could continue looking for a territory in which to live.

I went to the central fire as I was used to doing with my own people. And once again, people peeked out from their huts and stared at me. When I looked at them, they turned their heads away, or ducked their faces behind their long hair. The camp was quiet. I was used to a lot of noise in the mornings, people cooking, washing themselves, calling from tent to tent, children running and playing. And then it struck me, where were the children? I thought about yesterday, when I had first met them. Yes, there had been children, but very few. Perhaps there had been sickness here?

Someone brought me food and water. I ate and thought about what I needed to do.

As I sat there, poking bits of sticks into the flames, the silence settled on my shoulders like a heavy weight. I stood up and went in search of the woman from yesterday. When I found her, I held up an empty water skin. "My family is behind me, I will need to help them cross the dry land, but a huge wildcat guards the water." I made the sign for family, for travel, for water, for wildcat, for attack, and she looked at me, frowning, then finally nodded.

I still wasn't sure how much she had understood. With my hands and our bits of shared language, I tried to explain about my need for more water containers so I could return. She offered me clay jugs with wooden plugs that held more water than my skin bags. I thanked her then tied a skin over the back of black horse and then tied the jugs onto the skin. The woman also gave me a skin bag full of dried meat that I accepted gratefully. I was soon ready to leave.

One of the men who had led me to the camp yesterday came and stood beside me. I looked at him. He had a bow, a sleeping robe, a skin of water, and another bag tied across his back. He was obviously ready to go travelling. With me? I signed the question.

He nodded.

I shook my head. I didn't want someone with me.

He began to argue with his hands; he made the sign for help and for food. He wanted to help me, he could hunt, he gestured, and bring water. He looked at the woman and she looked at me and nodded. She said something to him. I realized, watching them together, and seeing how much they looked alike, that she must be his mother. She said something more to him and he nodded. She signed to me and I guessed she had told him to come along and help me.

I looked at him more closely. He was young, not much older than me; his hair was braided and tied back. His face had a kind of softness to it; he reminded me a bit of Lani. His eyes were pleading. There was obviously something he wanted to tell me but couldn't. Why on earth would he want to go with me?

"Name?" I asked in sign language.

"Dura," he said. He put his hand on his chest and then held out both hands to me in a sign of friendship. I stared at him some more. I really didn't want him to come but it would be much safer with him to help if we met another tiger or some other predator. Reluctantly I nodded. “I am Morven,” I answered, and all together, Dura and I, Black Horse and Spotted Dog, walked out of the camp. Dura’s people watched us go.

Chapter Five

The night after we left his people in their green valley, Dura and I camped on a high plateau overlooking the dry plains below. He was quick and competent. He made the fire, and gave me a handful of the dried meat his mother had packed for both of us. After I had eaten, I sat on ground with Spotted Dog beside me, both of us intent on the plain below. I was watching for other predators like the big cat, but nothing moved. When darkness covered the land, I rolled myself in my sleeping robe. But Dura sat beside the fire.

"I watch," he said. We had spent the day learning bits of each other's language.

"The dog will watch," I said. Dura went on sitting. He had turned to stare at me. "In my home," he said, "many men, few women."

The last thing I wanted to hear about were the problems of Dura's love life. I rolled over and turned my back, and fell asleep.

The next two days were spent enduring the fierce sun and heat that felt as if it wanted to suck any moisture from our bones and leave us as dried out skin-sacks on the ground. But eventually we saw the tops of the trees from a distance. As we came closer, I could smell smoke from cooking fires. I walked warily until I was sure these were my people. Then I began to run, despite my exhaustion and Dura plodded behind me.

The first thing I saw when I came into the line of trees was the skin of the giant cat stretched on a framework of branches. Several women were working at scraping it as we came into camp. They looked up as we came through the trees. The ground was trampled and dusty; the green pool in the centre of the trees was a muddy brown and all the fish were gone. Branches had been pulled off the trees to make shade and shelter. The place looked dead. The people weren't much better. They were thin and worn.

They all stopped what they were doing and crowded around us as we came into the camp. They had been watching us coming over the hot flat sand, and now they looked at us with hope in their eyes, but no one said anything. People stared at me, and at Dura. I was my usual strange self but these people, my clan, at least, were used to me. Dura was someone new to look at.

My mother stood still at the far side of the ring of tents. My sisters were holding on to her shirt, crowding behind her legs. Lani was standing beside her. I dropped the rope with which I was leading Black Horse and ran to her.

My mother ran and put her arms around me. "You are safe," she said. "I thought..." But she didn't say what she had thought. Instead, she pulled back. Her eyes narrowed. She looked me over. "And you have eaten. That means you have found somewhere safe. Have you found us a place with good food and water?"

I nodded, unsure of what to say. Yes, I found a place and no, I didn't think we could stay there for long. Best to get them all out of this wrecked place first.

"Three days journey," I said. "We will need water. There's nothing on the way." She nodded. Then she reached for me again and put her hand on my shoulder. I was surprised.

"You have done well," she said. Her face, always lined and worn, looked even more exhausted than I remembered. "Some are gone," she said. "Babies…elders." I nodded. I wanted to collapse by the fire, but there was much to do. I waved at the young man standing behind me. We had learned more of each other's language in the three long, hot, wearing days and nights of our journey.

"This is Dura," I said. "His people helped me. I think they will help the rest of us. I tried to tell them about our situation." I hesitated. "They are few, and the desert is large. They are in a valley with trees and water but beyond, more dry land, not as dry. We will only be able to stay there for a while."

She nodded. Then she said, "What is happening to the land, Morven? Once it sustained us so well, now the wind blows dust in our faces and the plants we need are gone. What shall we do? We have travelled so far." Her face was full of grief and shadows. I had never seen her like this. My mother was always so strong, so sure, always making decisions for everyone.

"We will find a better place," I said. "It can't be dry everywhere. We will find a green land for ourselves that will give us what we need." But in my heart, I had no idea if I spoke any kind of truth.

All this time, I had been conscious of Lani standing beside my mother. I couldn't bear to look at her face. I had left her without any farewell. I thought she must be very angry with me.

But now she just said quietly, "Yes, Morven, you have done well."

I looked at her. She smiled and held out her hands. "The only things that matters is that you are here, and safe."

I rested my head on her shoulder for a brief moment, then she helped me fetch water and food for the black horse and the spotted dog. Dura and I still had some of the dried meat we had brought with us. With that, and the few roots and plants that our mother had left, we made a kind of meal. There was little enough for each of us, and the children got most of it. We would need still more food to sustain us to cross the desert and then perhaps Dura's people would be able to assist us for a while until we had gathered our strength. But then we would have to move on again.

After we had eaten, my mother said, "Morven, you must speak to the people. Explain yourself. Tell them what you have found."

"No," I said. "I can't. You can tell them."

"You must tell them yourself. Give them hope. Give them a reason to keep going."

I shook my head but my mother held out her hand. "No, it is time you learned to speak in the Council for yourself."

I followed her to the central fire. People were beginning to gather. Nazar came and stood beside me and then Luz came from his tent and stood with us as well.

I looked into the faces of the people I had known all my life. I was silent. How could I talk? Where should I start? I began to shake all over as if I was facing the giant cat again.

Then anger rose in me. I had walked away from these people, from their laughter and their indifference. But some had helped. I looked at Luz and his wise dark eyes. I looked at and my mother and Lani, who were now sitting together in front of me and I decided to just talk to them.

"I left to find us a new place. I found this waterhole, and the giant cat. But three days more travel from here is a green valley. There are people there who will help us. We must carry as much water as we can, enough for three or four days."

The people listened but said little. I waited for questions but instead their questions were for Luz and Nazar. I felt shamed again. Why would they not talk to me?

They slowly dispersed back to their tents. There wasn't much to be decided. We were now in a situation where all we could do was go forward and try to help each other as much as we could.

In the morning, a group of the older hunters came to my mother's tent. I was sitting outside, cross-legged in the dust, making another grass rope. Lani sat beside me. The men stared at the spotted dog at my side and shook their heads. And at the black horse tied by my mother's tent, eating the bits of grass and tree branches we had found for him.

One of the men pointed at the black horse. "There is meat in this camp. There, waiting for us." The other men nodded. The black horse, peacefully chewing grass, was only meat to them. He wasn't a friend or a helper. My heart sank. I had no argument. I knew they were right, and yet I wanted to defend him as I would defend my mother, or a child. He was like a child in his behaviour. He depended on me to keep him fed and safe. And how could I argue with them when they wouldn't listen to me?

"No," Lani said suddenly. "He is more than that."

I stared at her. We all stared at her.

"Not meat," she added. "I have been thinking about this. He can be useful. He will carry the children. He will carry our burdens. He will help us all."

I considered. This was a new thought and it felt exciting, but also a thought I needed to toss around in my mind for a bit. Would it work? Would the children be safe? He had carried the water jugs for me without an argument. Why not children?

A few women at the other tents had overheard. An older woman named Suli came over to our tent. She had several children, some still young.

"I am so tired and the children are heavy. If this horse will carry children, I say, let him live." Her voice was shrill. Other people heard her raised voice and began to drift our way.

"We still have a bit of meat and other food," said my mother. "The thing we will need most is water."

I was thinking hard. The children were always a burden for all the people when we were moving. Everyone took turns, picked them up and carried them, until everyone was worn out and then it fell to the mothers or older children to carry them or they had to walk. The walking children got tired and then they stumbled along and fell behind and cried. Their mothers were always heavily burdened. There were the tents to carry, the sleeping robes, food, baskets, water bags, tools, digging sticks. Some of the men carried the heavier burdens but the women carried most of it. Mostly the older children carried the young children. The men usually used journeys as a time to hunt, or to range ahead and check out the new territory.

Lani looked at me. "Will he?" she asked.

"Yes," I said, sounding far more certain than I really was. "That is how it will be."

The men muttered and grumbled among themselves but they wouldn't go against the women's decision. They loved fresh meat. They were always unhappy when there were only roots and berries to eat.

When everything was packed and ready to go, I held the black horse while four of the smallest and frailest children were hoisted onto his back. He snorted and rolled his eyes and backed up. One of the children screamed which made him jump and a child fell off. I lifted them back on again, told them sternly to be quiet. Black Horse finally quieted and Lani walked beside the children to help hold them on. I tied some water bags together and hung them over his back as well. I led Black Horse. We went ahead and so we left the camp in a long line. This time even the spotted dog was carrying his own burden. I had tied two bags of dried roots over his back. He didn't like it either but he followed at my heels with his head down. Dura walked with the men but he carried our heavy bedrolls. And so we all left that place and moved forward again into a new land.

On the evening of the third day, when we staggered into Dura's village, we were all starved to the point of being just bones, and skin draped over the bones. We had travelled as fast as we could, not stopping for anything except to sleep, eat and then move on but we were alive. They came out of their tents and looked at us in horror. They shook their heads in distress and hurried to help. The camp smelled and sounded so familiar, smoke from the fires, people talking and laughing, and the wonderful smell of food. The women came towards us with their arms outstretched. They brought us food, enough to feed us all. That night, I crawled into a sleeping robe beside my mother, who had my little sisters tucked in beside her, and collapsed.

In the morning, they brought more food to our tents. They watched us eat. My mother and the woman I had met previously talked to each other as best they could. But the faces of these people looked worried as our people ate their food and I remembered how small the valley was and how difficult it would be to support so many hungry people.

In the next few days, our men went hunting. They caught deer and rabbits and groundhogs. They pulled fish from the creek as well, and the women hung them to dry. Dura's people looked worried but they were gracious and kind to us. As far as I could tell, they seemed to be gentle, but they had never travelled anywhere, and had met very few new people. They were fascinated by us, and perhaps, also afraid.

Dura came to my mother's fire some nights, but one night I saw him sitting with Lani. From that night on, he spent more and more time with her. He was at her fire at night and during the day. Sometimes he sat staring at her while she ducked her head so her hair fell over her face.

The black horse began to recover his strength as well, tearing hungrily at the tall grass along the creek. He had worked hard, carrying a load of children. Everyone agreed that this idea of Lani's had been a good one. They seemed to forget that catching Black Horse had been my idea, and my doing. I was angry at the people who ignored me but happy about Lani and Dura. Dura's fumbled hints to me during our trip had been unwelcome.

The spotted dog hunted every day and our people began to laugh again, to tell stories. The children ran and played together and splashed in the creek. The men continued to hunt and bring in game. For a space of time, we lived in peace and plenty, the way we had once lived. But we knew we couldn't stay, and therefore the rest and the peace were like clear water poured onto sand.

It was obvious that we were quickly using up the valley and what it had to offer. Everything became scarce: firewood, animals, roots, berries. We used them all. We had to. We had to fatten up for the next ordeal. We had no idea when we would rest again. All we knew is that the land ahead of us was dry and that our travelling would be difficult.

Dura's people began to mutter among themselves. Who could blame them? They had a safe home and we were ruining it. The land would not support so many people. The women were using this opportunity to mend tents, clothes, baskets and to make new things. They worked all the time. Lani was always among them. I was not.

Actually, I was restless. No one needed me for anything and no one paid attention to me. I wandered on the black horse, the spotted dog at our side. He had grown and gained weight on the good food in this new camp. He was no longer a half-grown pup but a full-grown dog and a big one. Perhaps it was the extra food or the lack of competition from other dogs but he was taller than most dogs; his head was almost at my waist when we walked. He lay beside me at night and walked beside me all day except when he took himself off to go hunting.

I went far into the dry grassy hills beyond the valley. I was hoping for signs of water, perhaps another valley, another refuge, but no such thing appeared. Instead, there were endless rolling hills covered with dry grass, low trees, and patches of thorny brush that scratched and caught at my clothing. It wasn't desert; more like a huge dry plain.

We would need to carry as much water as we could. I had already gone south, to where the creek from the valley disappeared into the sands of the desert. But the creek flowed from the north; creeks, we knew, often came from lakes or mountains. So it made some sense to go towards the source of the creek.

One late afternoon, as I was returning from wandering, I heard a strange thin distant cry. Spotted Dog stopped and sniffed the air and when he set off through the brush, I followed. We climbed a hill we hadn't climbed before. The top of the hill was covered with large black rocks, one of which was flat. And on top of this rock, was a tiny baby, wrapped in a hide with its face covered.

It was a very young baby, only a few days old. I picked it up and it quieted, perhaps thinking I would feed it. It was a thin tiny thing, its feeble hands waving in the air. I couldn't understand what it was doing there.

I tucked it under my arm and went back down to the camp. The camp went dead silent with they saw me coming. I took the baby to my mother. When I showed her what I had found, her face creased in anguish.

"Now I understand," she said very quietly, so only I could hear. "They kill their own children. That is how they survive here. I wondered why there were so few children." She looked at me. "We must go now, Morven. We can't stay here. This is a sad, terrible place. Killing children is too high a price to pay for being safe and fed."

She tucked the baby under her robe and let it suckle. She still had milk from her last child. Dura's people had all disappeared into their huts.

And then one woman came creeping from a hut, walked toward my mother, with her head down, dragging her feet in the dust. Tears were rolling down her dusty face. She held out her arms and my mother placed the tiny baby in her arms. She hugged it to her and began to wail. And then she handed it back to my mother and ran back to her hut.

Before we left, my mother went and talked to the elders of Dura's people and invited them to come with us. She didn't say anything about the baby. She simply talked about how good it would be to find a place where no one would have to worry about a lack of food. But they had been in the valley too long; it was all they knew and they wouldn't, or couldn't, leave.

Lani had shuddered when she found out about the baby that had been left to die. She was excited and hopeful for her own child, now that her belly had started to swell.

"We will find a new land, Morven," Lani said. "We will find a place to stay and where our children will grow fat. Perhaps then, you too will have a child."

I shrugged. I didn't want a child. I had seen enough of the work and the burdens that children brought to my mother and the other women.

Dura seemed happy with Lani, and she was happy with him. He spent much of his time now with the men of our people. He had learned our language.

I saw his mother watching him with a sad face. Dura had told Lani he would come with us when we left. Once more, we packed our tents and sleeping robes and stores of food. Once again, the poor black horse was loaded down with children. I had the idea of tying a hide on his back to make it easier for them to stay on; Lani fashioned straps for them to hold onto.

On the morning we left, the camp of Dura's people was silent. Everyone stayed inside and didn't watch us go. I think they were ashamed. They had been kind. They were gentle people and afraid for us and for themselves but how they lived now horrified us, and they knew it.

We walked all that day and by evening, we had reached a sheltered valley in the hills. We were still following the creek so there was no shortage of water, plus the men had hunted all day. They found small game, and the women found plants and berries. We travelled that day and the next and the next and the land grew flatter and drier but still, there were pockets of green, small canyons full of trees and brush, places animals thrived. Travelling was dull work; exhausting and full of small irritations. It was a constant effort to keep fed, warm, to keep everyone together and all the necessary tools and pieces for a successful camp.

The black horse seemed to have grown used to his burden of children; the children had given him a new name, Akal, and they played with him as they would another child. Some of them also played with the spotted dog and since he was friendly they also began to play with some of the other dogs and ceased to throw stones at them. So travelling was tedious but peaceful.

More and more, I began to love this land we were passing through. I loved the huge blue bowl of sky; so wide, constantly changing, clouds passing overhead, purple shadows on the yellow rolling plain. I loved the way the grass waved, changing colour as the wind beat at it. I loved the many colours of the hills: brown, red, purple, and green where there was water. Something in all this vastness spoke to me. I was happy in a way I had never been before.

And I was much happier in my clan. The people had respect for me. I had a friend in Lani. All was well.

Until one day when we were coming down a long slope towards a pool of water. We were in a valley that was like a large, grassy drum. The black horse threw up his head, jumped and called out. I saw them on the other side of the valley, black shapes. I could hear them call back. Black Horse whirled around me in a circle. A couple of the children fell off, the older ones slid off, and the smaller ones howled. The mothers came running. All the dogs barked.

Black Horse jumped away from me; he pulled and pulled at the grass rope with which I was trying to hold him until it broke. And then, suddenly, he was free. He ran, kicking his heels over his head, and jumping. Bundles and bags flew from his back. I stared after him, open-mouthed. And hurt. Wasn't he my child, my family? I had gotten used to thinking of him this way. He charged across the valley bowl until he was only a black speck joining the others, Together they disappeared over the rim of the hill.

I picked up the broken rope and looked around. Everyone was staring at me, including Lani.

"Where is your hairy man now?" one of the young men called. "Perhaps he has heard another woman more to his taste calling him and has gone to find her."

Lani asked, "Oh, no, Morven. What can you do?"

I stared at her. I had no idea what to do. The children were still crying. Hides and packages were scattered on the ground. Some of the women bent to pick them up, muttering at me, and giving me nasty looks.

I was still trying to figure out what had happened. I took the rope and trotted after the black horse. I could hear the people laughing behind me. I put my head down and ran harder. So much for my speech to the people about Black Horse being such a helper. Now they would they think of me as someone who couldn't keep her promises. I ran faster. When I came over the edge of the far hill, there he was, my friend, crowded in with others of his kind, snorting, bending heads, blowing air at each other, and occasionally squealing and tossing heads.

My foot clinked on a stone, one of them heard me, threw up its head and, suddenly, in a flash of dust and thunder, they were all gone.

I had lost him. I couldn't think what to do. Finally, I turned and went back to my own people. The spotted dog came and licked my hand. Together we trudged into camp. The people had evidently decided to stop for the day. Women were putting up tents, gathering firewood and lighting fires. There would soon be warmth and food and comfort, none of which I wanted at the moment. I was angry, but wasn't sure at what. At Black Horse for running away? At my own carelessness? At the people who still laughed at me no matter how hard I tried to do the right thing?

The men were standing together, muttering. They stopped talking when they saw me. But I didn't have to hear them to know what they were thinking. They were thinking of hunting these horses.

Hunting, meat, the excitement and swagger of a successful hunt, the women happy, the children stuffed to bursting. This would be a big hunt; food for many days, even weeks. We would be able to stay in one place for a while, cure hides, make new tents and clothes, repair footwear. Children would grow; Lani's child would be born healthy. There was nothing about any of this with which I could disagree.

Except that in our days and weeks of living together, somehow the black horse really had become my family. And that meant that his relatives were also my family. And that meant once again pitting myself against the will of my family, my relatives, my clan, my people. I had been in this same position before and I had managed to persuade the men to think at least a little differently. But there was nothing I could I tell them now that would persuade them not to hunt these horses.

I went towards my mother's tent. She handed me a water hide. "Water," she said tersely. I fetched the water, I helped her put up the tent, I sat with my small sisters and helped them eat. And then I went to find Lani. She was sitting by her own fire, working as always, strips of leather in her lap, braiding a new rope for me to replace the broken one.

We sat together in silence. I always felt better near Lani. She always knew what I was thinking, and she usually had something to tell me that was useful.

"I'm sorry you lost your friend," she said finally. "Now the men will want to eat him. They will finally get their chance."

I only nodded.

"But I've been thinking."

I nodded again.

"The women have been talking."

I was sure they had been talking—about me, laughing and jeering at how foolish I had been.

"They are wondering why there is only one horse to help us. Why don't we have more?"

I stared at her. What was she asking about?

"It has been good for everyone to have some help with the burdens and especially the children. It would be even more help if we had more horses; the tents are such a weight for all of us, plus the food. No wonder the women grow bent and tired, carrying such loads. When we could stay in one place for a while, it didn't matter. But now travelling, the women are worn out. Their feet hurt. Their backs hurt. We want more horses. Can you get them?"

I was still staring. Getting Black Horse to be my friend had been an accident because I wanted to spite the men and I had wanted to save the horses. But to get more? Could that be done? How could it be done? I had no idea. Could I get them?

"Maybe," I said.

She handed me the rope she had made and smiled. It was long, made of carefully braided strips of cured deer hide. "That will be a great gift to your people," she said. "We will sing songs about you and your gift."

I stared into the fire for a while and then I stood up, slung the rope over my shoulder, and left. I needed to think.

Around me I could hear the usual noises of the camp, babies being sung to and rocked to sleep, the old men around one fire and the old women around another, the younger girls working and talking, the younger boys laughing and jeering at each other. Gradually it would all go quiet as people drifted to sleep.

I went past the firelight, into the shadows, and beyond the camp to where the dogs made their own camp. Sometimes Spotted Dog slept with me; other times he slept with his own kind. I did the same. I felt at home with the dogs now that Spotted Dog had become my friend; the dogs dug holes in the sandy ground to sleep, and they were always glad to move over and let me curl up with them. With a dog or two at my back, and another one curled at my belly, I would stay warm all night. Often I brought a hide with me, but sometimes I simply curled up in the dust. Tonight when I sat down, one of the older females came to my side. She grunted as she flopped down. I rubbed her head and back. She was heavy and her sides heaved and moved as she lay there. Her puppies would be born soon. Dogs with puppies stayed behind when the camp moved. I often wondered what happened to them.

The other dogs wandered over. They seemed to like attention. They were always curious about what I was doing and often I brought bits of food along with me and shared it with them all so now they were always excited to see me.

Eventually I left the dogs and went back to the camp. I wanted my own bed, I wanted to curl up in the darkness of the tent and sleep without dreaming. The question Lani had asked was bothering me because I didn't actually have answer for her or any idea how to get more horses.

And then a man stepped out of the shadows of a small tree. "Morven," he said. It was Dura. "I am sorry you lost your friend. I am sure he will come back."

I didn't say anything. I didn't want to talk to anyone. I needed to think. I waited for him to go but he stood patiently, his head bowed. It was this quality about him that I liked and that also annoyed me, his ability to wait, to be patient and gentle. His people were like that too. That is why they had trapped themselves in that one small valley. I still wondered why they had stayed. They could have come with us. We could have joined our clans together and become stronger. But they had refused.

"Morven, the men have asked me to talk with you. They would like you to come to their fire. They have a question for you."

Dura had easily been accepted as one of the men of our clan. According to Lani, they liked him because he was a good hunter, a hard worker, generous and easygoing. He had been accepted so easily and yet I remained an outsider.

I hesitated. Why should I talk to them? They probably wanted me to show them where the black horse had gone so they could kill him. Or even more likely, they wanted me to stay in the camp while they went hunting so they would be sure I didn't interfere.

I nodded, followed Dura around the camp to the men's fire, came into the circle of firelight, and sat down.

One of the older men nodded to Dura but no one acknowledged me. Except my uncle, Nazar, who nodded to me and smiled. This is foolish, I thought. I could be sleeping somewhere, not wasting my time with the men. But I waited. I couldn't, without being completely rude, just get up and leave. I looked around the circle. I had never come to the men's circle before. The men were all familiar, but it felt different sitting at their fire. It made me feel uneasy. I wasn't sure what to expect. Sometimes men spent time with the women and their children; sometimes a man and a woman lived together for a while. But the women had their ways and customs and the men had theirs. Mostly the women looked after the children and the care of the children. Men looked after the care and protection of the whole clan. I had always resented the men because they wouldn't let me hunt with them, because they made fun of me, because when our people moved, the hunters went ahead, unburdened, while the women struggled along carrying bales and bags and children.

These men ranged in age. Usually boys left their mothers and went to live in the men's tents when they began wanting to have sex with girls. Several of the men were elders; their hair hung down in long, grey braids. Finally, the oldest man, whose name was Jalal, and who often spent time at my mother's fire, looked at me. Jalal had black eyes that were so set back under shaggy eyebrows, it looked like they were almost closed. I looked at him and then I looked away.

"Morven," he said now. "We have been watching you. We would like to know how you do what you do with that black horse. We would like to do this as well. We would like to know your secret."

I was astonished for the second time that night. First, the women, now the men. They hadn't been laughing at me after all, at least not this time.

"We have been talking about this. It seems to us that you have added the horse's strength to your own. This makes you fast and strong. Faster and stronger than us. Some of us thought you were becoming a shaman, that you used magic to trick the horses. But instead I see you talking and being patient, spending time to learn their ways. I think this is something we could learn from you. And we are also afraid now that as we travel, we may find others who are not so happy with our coming. If we had the strength and speed that you have, they might be afraid of us. If we had the strength and speed of horses, we could travel when we needed to find water and food. We have talked and thought about this a great deal."

Now they looked at me. They leaned forward, waiting for my answer. I didn't have one, but I had to think of something.

"Being with the black horse is like speaking without words," I said finally. "First I learned a language of hunger, and then a language of running. And then a language of pushing and pulling. And then he became like my child." I paused. "Until today," I said. "He has gone to find others of his kind."

They nodded.

"But if his kind lived with us, and among us, then he would have no need to run away," said Nazar. "We would have more horses. We could eat some and keep the others to help us. We would all be fast and strong. The women would have help. This is a good thing."

This was also a new thought and a good one. I sat in silence while the shape of it formed in my head.

But how could we compel them to come and live among us? I had compelled Black Horse with food, and then with the rope. I had pushed and pulled at him without really thinking about it. I wanted to go somewhere and he had followed. Then he had lost his other family and had only me. Until now.

Would he come back again? Perhaps I had given up too easily.

"Tomorrow," I said, without really thinking about what I was saying, "perhaps I could follow this new clan of horses. I could see where they go. I will live among them and I will try to make a plan that will let me bring some horses to live with us. I have to think about this. When I know what I am going to do, I will come and tell you."

The men nodded.

"We will wait here for you for a few days," Jalal said. "But then we must move on and to do that, we need food. If you are not back, we will go hunting the horses."

I got to my feet and left the men's fire, my head buzzing.

Chapter Six

I was hungry, I was tired, and I was very hot. I was also, I had decided, an idiot to agree to take on this task of catching wild horses. Sweat dripped and ran, stinging my eyes. I wiped it away and trudged on.

I had been following the black horse and his new family for days. But I was only a nuisance to them. When they saw me, they moved away, but not very far. They would only allow me to come close enough to see them, not close enough to touch, not close enough to actually convince them I was harmless. And there was nothing they needed; the grass in the various small valleys was rich and full, they had water when they wanted it. Their leader was a grey mare, old and wise. She wasn't afraid of me. She just wanted me to go away. Sometimes she would leave the others and charge towards me, ears back and teeth bared. And then she would turn and leave.

But still I followed and still, they moved on. At least they led me to water, but every day, I had to take enough time to hunt for food, dig roots, pick berries, snare some small animal and make a fire. While I did that, they would move off and the next day I would have to search for them again. I was getting nowhere.

I was worn down, and missed my mother and the warmth of her fire. I missed being soft and comfortable in the sleeping robes in the tent at night with the small ones curled around me, feet poking me in the back and head. I missed food appearing with no effort from me. And I mostly missed Lani, her wise, smiling brown eyes. I even missed Dura, though why that should be I couldn't tell.

I had made the spotted dog stay with the camp. I yelled at him and threw stones to make him stay and I could tell he was hurt and confused. But I had thought that having him around would make catching the horses even harder. Instead, not having him was a problem. He would have told me, with his ears and nose, where the horses had gone. He would have helped me find food and kept me warm at night. I had made yet another mistake. I was doing everything wrong on this strange journey. I had told the men I would try, and I was trying, and every day it was becoming more obvious that all my efforts were accomplishing nothing. I had no plan at all other than to keep going.

I came over a hill and there was the horse herd below me, in a small narrow valley beside another creek. Good grazing in this dry and rolling land was mostly beside the creeks and in small valleys and deep canyons, where there were springs and where the hot sun didn't dry everything up. They were pulling hungrily at the grass. Because I kept them moving, I hadn't given them enough time to eat and they were getting thin. Every day the sun rose a little higher and the land became dryer and hotter. The horses never went too far from the creek or from the small streams that fed it, tumbling down from springs among the hills.

It was a strange land, dry and sparse and yet, abundant in places. I was learning the land as I travelled; the dry flat tablelands that seemed to stretch on forever, the rocky ravines and canyons where there was brush and water and game. The land looked barren and dry until I looked closer, and now I was beginning to understand that there were hidden places that would feed and shelter me. I was learning to feel at home here.

It was almost evening. The sun slanted in long dusty arrows over the hill and onto the grass and horses below, so that they glowed golden and shining. I squatted on my heels just below the brow of the hill. The horses paid no attention, and for once I paid no attention to them. I was sick of them and sick of myself: my sweat, my smell, my failure.

I went down the hill with my head down, and slouched past them to the creek. They moved away, but only a little.

I took off my hide wrapper and slid into the water, lay and stretched and rolled in its icy coolness, then came out, moved down the creek to a grove of willow, and made a fire. I dug some reeds and cut off the roots, caught a couple of small fish, dug some sunflower roots, wrapped it all in wet leaves and put it in the ashes. I dug a hole in the sandy bank, laid my wrapper inside and then curled up, with my head on my arms. After a while, I stood up, went to the fire, fished out the food and ate. It was dull stuff without salt. My people had once traded for salt, but we hadn't had any for a long time, since we had left our familiar territory and our familiar trade routes. Salt cured meat and hides, as well as made food taste better.

I wondered what the horses did for salt. All wild animals would go a long way for a taste of salt. The horses might come to me for salt. But where could I find salt to give them?

I crouched beside the small fire, miserable and feeling sorry for myself and then I curled myself in my wrapper, wriggled my hips for comfort into the sandy hole I had dug, and slept.

It was very dark when I woke again. Something had disturbed me, a noise, a footstep, perhaps a predator. I had a knife and a bow but these would be of little use against a tiger or bear. There it was again: a shuffle, a thud. I knew that sound well. It was the sound of a hoof against stone. I sat up very slowly. They were all around me, grazing. I could hear teeth tearing grass, the muted thump and shuffle of feet, the occasional snort or deep sigh. Without thinking, I had camped near the tall grass by the creek. They had come to eat while I was sleeping, and thus was no threat to them.

I could see their shapes outlined against the stars. After a while, I figured out which one was him. Very slowly and carefully, I stood up. They didn't seem to notice. I drifted, step by step, through the press of warm dark bodies towards the black horse, who stuck his nose out at me in greeting, licked the salt off my arm and went back to grazing. I went back to my hole. Several of the horses came and sniffed at me, snorted, but didn't run away. I dozed but didn't sleep. As the dawn sky was beginning to lighten, birds began to sing from the thick brush along the creek. I heard a horse snort and a few minutes later, they all began to leave, forming into a line and climbing the hill out of the creek valley. Quickly, I grabbed all my things and followed. I fell into line behind the last horse.

All day I continued to follow them. Something had changed. They had stopped being afraid of me. Perhaps they had come close enough to see I was no predator, no threat.

I tried to prove my good intentions. When they lay down on the grass in the warm sun, I lay down as well. When they grazed, I sat on the grass and put bits of it in my mouth. Eventually, some of the younger ones came and sniffed at me and we blew at each other. The grey mare chased them off but they came back. I shook my head at them in play, and finally, we ran and chased each other.

All morning, we drifted together, slowly south over the flat plains, while they ate and my belly rang with hunger. At noon, we went into a valley, to the creek, and everyone lined up for a drink.

Then the younger horses played, the foals had a drink, the older mares stood apart under trees with their heads together, swishing their tails at flies.

I went upstream and speared some fish, found some roots and built a fire with which to cook. When the shadows under the trees began to lengthen, I gathered my things and went back to the horse herd. When they saw me, they began to move south again. All night we drifted slowly together, them snatching at grass but always moving, always moving, step by step. I was hoping they would slowly move back to the area where I thought the camp must be. And all the while, in the dark, under the bright stars, moving and stepping by starlight, I was planning in my head what must be done.

By the next day, I thought we had gone far enough. The shape of the hills, the stones, the bent grass, told me I had come this way before. I left the horses and trotted towards the camp as fast as I could. The visions of what to do shaped themselves in my head. I knew this could be done. I could see it so clearly in my head, the work that would bring my vision into being.

But as soon as I came within the line of tents, I knew something was wrong.

No one looked at me. People turned their faces away.

My heart swelled; I began to run towards my mother's tent. As soon as I saw the women sitting outside with the small children beside them, I knew. I stooped and lifted the tent flap. It was dim inside, the familiar half-light of the tent, along with the smell of smoke and food and warmth and comfort, everything the tent had always meant for me, no matter how far I travelled or how strange I became.

But my mother's body was lying motionless on a pallet of furs and skins. She would never greet me again. She hadn't been dead very long. I was used to seeing dead animals and I knew right away she had been dead only for a couple of days. It was strange to see her, this body that was my mother and not my mother. I sat down beside her; I took her cold stiff hand and held it to my face and sniffed the familiar odour of her skin that still lingered. I looked at her hand with its thin worn fingers. How hard she had worked, my mother, how much she had cared, and what an ungrateful daughter I had been. Tears rolled down my face. I held my mother's hand and rocked back and forth. My throat hurt. I began to wail.

The tent flap lifted and Lani came in. She folded herself down to sit beside me. I leaned my head against her and we wept together, raising our voices together in wailing for my mother.

Later, we would bury my mother with her bone and bead jewelry and her clay pots and her skins and furs. Later, we would burn the tent and then make a new one. It would all be a lot of work. Finally, I stopped crying and I leaned against Lani, weary to the depths of my bones. The spotted dog nosed his way into the tent and came behind me, licked my face and wiggled his delight at seeing me.

"She was digging," Lani said. "It was hot, too hot and she fell. We brought her inside, gave her water, but she didn't recover. This trip has been too hard for all of us. The children are so thin. We need to find a place, soon, that we can settle."

I nodded. It would be up to me now, the digging, the cooking, the sewing, feeding my two little sisters. Soon I would be as worn and thin as my mother, doing the work I hated, that must be done. I would have to forget about the horses now. There wouldn't be time for them.

"Come," said Lani. "There is food at our fire. Not much, but enough."

That night, as I sat at Lani's fire, Nazar came to me. He sat beside me, and again I wept, and he wept with me.

"Luz wishes to talk to you," he finally said, when our grief was still. Luz the shaman.

I felt my insides twist but there was no way to refuse a request from the shaman. I followed my uncle through the camp to the shaman's tent. My uncle lifted the flap and I ducked inside.

It was hot in the tent. A small fire was burning and the tent was full of smoke. It was almost impossible to see. My eyes watered. I coughed and choked and then recovered enough to see the old man across the fire, his eyes peering out from behind his tangled hair.

I waited.

"I will miss your mother," Luz said finally. "She was a leader among our people. She was kind and strong and she cared for all of us."

I felt tears in my eyes and squeezed them back.

"And what about you? Who will you become now?" he asked.

I had no answer to this.

He chuckled. "Will you now become a woman among the women, will you take your place and learn to cook and weave and sew and bear children? Will you carry burdens, like the horse you lost? When you get old, will you sit by the fire and gossip with your friend Lani until your days are done?" And then he answered his own question. "No, I don't think so."

He leaned forward and threw a handful of twisted grass on the fire so it blazed up momentarily. "Can you see a different path before you, red-headed Morven?" His voice croaked. "You have been walking your own way since you were born. Where will your path lead you now? Will you go ahead of the people and lead them into a new future? Or will you go alone into a new place? " He threw more grass on the fire. "I see many tangled paths together. Will you choose for us, or for yourself?"

I felt dizzy from the smoke and from his questions. I didn't know what I was being asked to choose or even how to choose. But I leaned forward and looked at him as clearly as I could.

"I will do my best for the people and for my family," I said, "and I will follow my own path where it leads."

For some reason, he found this funny. He threw back his head and laughed. Then he waved his hand in dismissal. "Then you will always be a person with two heads and a divided heart. But perhaps you are strong enough to live that way. Go with care, young Morven. Your mother watches over you, and I will always be here waiting for you."

I missed my mother. Was she really watching me? Was she angry that I had been gone when she died? The shaman taught us that the spirits of the people who died went to another land next to this one but that they could still see us.

My mother once told me, "Morven, the dead go into another world. We know this is true because our shaman, Luz, can travel there and meet with them."

Once out of the tent, I gulped down huge breaths of clean cold air. My head cleared. The shaman was only a strange, wizened old man in a dark tent. I had things to do. I shook my head and went back to Lani's fire.

Chapter Seven

"New people," Lani whispered to me. "What will they be like?"

Some of the men out hunting had brought word that morning that they had spotted a settlement, not just tents, but strange places with walls, places unlike anything they had seen before. They had come back to the camp to talk about it. These people might be like Dura's people, friendly and gentle. Or perhaps not.

That night we held a council. It was Luz who suggested I should be the one to go ahead and meet the people first, to feel them out, see if they had food, see if we could stay with them for a while. This surprised everyone. The men were angry. They thought a group of them should go. The women were angry as well because they thought we should send a group of our elder men and women.

But Luz pointed out that I had done a good job of meeting Dura's people and persuading them to help us. This quieted everyone. And no one ever really argued with Luz. I asked Lani to come with me. If these new people were friendly, then the attitude of their women would tell us. If they offered us food, and help, we would tell them there were more of us. If not, we would leave again.

Now we were crouched on a hill, watching the people below us go about their work.

We knew already they were different from us. Their dwellings had stone walls and wooden frames. They had animals in pens. From the depth of the trails around their houses, it looked like they had been there for a while. From a distance, the people all looked well-fed and healthy. They came and went from each other's houses. We could hear their voices calling, lifted like bird cries in the soft morning air.

We stood up and moved slowly down the slope. Their dogs saw us first and came running, barking and growling. Spotted Dog ran in front of us, making the same noises right back.

Two women came ahead of the others. We four looked at each other from a distance. Their black hair was shining and done up in braids. Their cheeks were round and red and their dark eyes sparkled. Their faces were different from those of my people, their eyes rounder, and without sharp cheekbones.

When I looked at them, I was suddenly aware of the stained and torn hide that was wrapped around me, that my hair was long, unbraided, and falling in my eyes, that my feet were bare, that the ribs stood out under Spotted Dog's hide.

We stood still and they came slowly towards us holding out their hands in a gesture of welcome. We lowered our eyes and our heads and held out our hands as well. After all, we were the ones asking for help and kindness.

When they came up beside us, they asked us questions in their soft, guttural language, which neither Lani nor I could understand. But they understood our skinny arms, and the torn hides around us. When they gestured for us to come, we followed. We stared around us as we came into their camp. I noticed the smells first, the smell of animals in pens, the smell of many people together, the smell of smoke, the smell of food cooking.

They showed us into a small hut, dark and smoky. When our eyes adjusted, we could see, across the fire, two people, ancient looking, their skin wrinkled and sagging. They were wrapped in blankets made, not of hides but of something we didn't recognize, something made somehow in bright colours. One of them—I thought she was a woman but I wasn't sure—leaned forward and placed several bundles of braided grass on the fire. The flames leapt up and we could see it was a woman and a man. They gestured for us to sit.

They said nothing, simply stared at us. Finally the woman's hands moved in a kind of sign language, a little bit like our trade language, asking, I guessed, where we had come from.

I pointed back, in the direction from which we had come. She stared some more. Then she stood up, came around the fire, put her wrinkled hands on my head. She grabbed a piece of my hair and tugged and then patted my cheek. Then she leaned forward, stared at Lani, poked her swollen belly, and laughed. She stroked Lani's cheek as well, then walked around us, said something to the old man who also laughed. I hadn't thought there was anything funny about us at all. And I really, really hated being laughed at.

The old woman snapped out a loud stream of language and two women came back into the tent. They leaned forward, took Lani's arms, gestured for her to go with them and led her out of the tent.

"No," I started to say, and stood up, but Lani was already gone.

The old woman gestured at me to sit back down and then sat back down herself, beside the old man. I sat, although I was uneasy. I wanted to run after Lani, see where they had taken her.

The old woman pointed at me, at my hair. She began to talk in a language I couldn't understand. But as she talked, the sweet smoke from the fire clogged my eyes and throat. I closed my eyes and suddenly, whatever language she was using began to make an odd sense. I couldn't understand it but I could see it. I didn't understand what was happening.

Bright colours flashed in my head and then the colours resolved themselves into pictures, pictures I could see but couldn't understand, men fighting, and then horses running. A woman was weeping; she looked like Lani and fear suddenly choked me. Then birds flew overhead, huge birds with giant wings and cruel eyes; they flew down at the fighting men and attacked them. And then giant dogs attacked the birds and drove them away.

And then suddenly, all was peace on the plains, the sun shone, the grass was many colours. Each blade of grass was its own colour and shone with inner light. It was all so real that when I finally forced my eyes open, I was shocked to find myself still in the smoky hut. The old woman leaned forward. She flicked her hands towards my face, flicking more smoke at me. She babbled at me in her language. Her voice was irritating, high and screechy. She was trying to tell me something, something urgent. But by now I had had enough.

"Thank you," I said, putting my hands together in a gesture of thanks. I bowed forward. "But my friend and I are hungry and tired." My hands flashed. "We have come far," I signed, in trade language, hoping they would understand.

Both the old man and the old woman nodded and laughed and screeched at me some more. They waved, indicating I should go.

I came out of the hut into the evening dusk. It had been late afternoon when we went in. Lani was sitting beside the fire with the other women. She looked fine, not frightened. I looked at Lani, bewildered.

"Come and sit," she said. "They will bring you food."

"How long was I in there?" I asked her.

"I don't know," she said. "Quite a while. I was starting to worry."

"Were you out here the whole time?"

"Yes, of course."

We stopped talking because a young woman had approached us. "Shuz," she said, pointing to herself. She motioned for us to follow her. She took us to one of the wooden houses. There were strange beds in it, made of wood and raised off the floor and piled high with hides. She ducked out again and came back with two wooden bowls of food. I was impressed with both the bowls and the food. The food was meat and greens and some kinds of seeds, spiced with some seasoning I didn't recognize. The bowls had been carved out of wood with great care. After I cleaned up the food, I turned over my bowl and admired the work that had gone into it. Obviously, these people had the time to sit around and make beautiful things.

Shuz came back and took our bowls out. She didn't look at us, although when we tried to thank her for our food, she gave us a shy smile, looking up from under her mass of black hair. Lani and I looked at each other. So far these people seemed mostly friendly. In fact, we hadn't seen enough of them to really tell. But my strange experience with the old man and old woman bothered me. Had it been some kind of test? Something in the smoke? I told Lani about it and she shrugged.

"They have welcomed us," she said. "They will give us food. That is the important thing right now."

At first light, we rose and went to the creek to pee and wash and drink water. When we came back to the camp, the central fire was burning; a woman was bent over tending it. Shuz again. Did she do all the work of this camp? At least she smiled at us.

She gave us hot water to drink in clay cups, and then the two women we had met yesterday came to us. We showed them with signs that there were more of us. They nodded. They had sent out scouts to look for us. We tried to ask permission to bring the rest of our people to their camp. They looked at each other. I couldn't read that glance.

Finally, one of them nodded and waved at us to go. I wasn't really sure what she understood, but I took her hand wave as an excuse to go. As I trotted out of the camp, I noticed they had animals, fuzzy grey, with horns, fastened in places made of logs laid on top of one another and tied with ropes. Shuz was standing in one of the pens. She watched me go but didn't wave.

Lani and I found our people where we had left them. They were already packed and eager to move. Eventually, we all straggled into the camp of these new people, and a sad, torn and ragged bunch we were.

We made our camp beside their camp, and they brought us food, strange foods we hadn't eaten before. They took milk from the animals in the pens. The animals stunk but their milk tasted good and the children in particular gulped it down.

We tried to tell them how far we had come but they shook their heads. It was obvious they didn't travel; how could they travel with such heavy wood and stone houses and so many animals? Their children and our children stared and pointed and giggled but it didn't take long before they were playing together. That night, we slept with full bellies.

Over the next few days, we established our own camp close to that of these new people although not really with them. We kept our two camps separate. But we began to visit back and forth, to learn their language and their strange ways. Gradually, over the next few days, we figured out that the place where they lived was called Kazaan, and they had been there, they said, forever.

This was strange to us, for our people had always wandered, but within the same familiar, circular routes. We would stay in one place for while, until we had used all the food plants in that area and caught the game. We followed the plants, and the animals in various seasons, or at least, we had, until the land betrayed us. These people took their animals out every day, and wandered with them, but brought them back at night. Their horned animals were called sheep and goats. They hunted as well, and the women gathered plants, as we did, but they also made clothes from the hair and wool they took from their animals. They drank the milk as well.

In return, the people of Kazaan cared for these animals and kept them safe. It was like the bargain I had once had with the black horse, before he left me. These people hunted horses for food. I wondered what they would say if they saw me with Black Horse and his family, if they saw me on the back of Black Horse, taller and stronger and faster than they could ever be.

Being here made my life easier. I gave over responsibility for my younger sisters to Lani and her sisters and her mother. I was too impatient with them; I lost my temper when they started wailing for our mother. Lani was gentle and kind and when she offered to take them into her tent, I accepted.

Instead, I began to spend time with the women who herded the flocks and tended them. I spent most of my time with the woman named Shuz, and worked at becoming her friend. It took a while. She was shy and mistrustful, but one morning I followed her to the pens where she was looking after wooly animals. She took them out during the day to graze, so one morning, I followed her, spent the day with her watching the sheep graze, sitting on a rocky hill looking out over the blue-shadowed plain. I began to point and ask her the names of things. After that, I spent days wandering behind the herds over the flat plain while we learned each other's languages. Shuz taught me much. She taught me about the land, the plants they used, the weather, the animals, what lived where. It was good knowledge. She was clever with the animals. The sheep followed her as if she was one of them, and she looked a bit like the sheep as well. She had a long face, and black matted hair, which she often pulled forward when we came into camp. I liked her because she didn't look at me with suspicion, as some of the other others of her clan did. Although, most of the Kazaans were friendly.

From her, I learned to build the pens and shelters where the Kazaans kept their animals. I helped to treat them when they were ill. I learned to get the milk in the evening; I learned how the milk turned into many new foods, rich foods, and I saw how the wool and hair from the sheep and goats were turned into clothes and blankets.

Our people were so happy to be in one place for a while; the children no longer cried at night, people began to sing and tell stories around their fires again.

One night, a family decided to host a dance. Most of our drums had been left behind but there were enough small drums to hold the beat for the dance. Everyone was glad to gather, to sing, and laugh. People danced, weaving in and out of a circle. I stayed on the edge of the firelight for a while, watching. Several of the Kazaan people had come, drawn by the songs and the drums. Our people shared food, showed them our dances.

Finally, the beat of the drum pulled me into the circle. At first I stomped around on the edge, quietly, but something about the drum and the people singing and the relief we were all feeling together made me happier than I remembered feeling for a long, long time.

And while I danced, people smiled at me and I heard people saying my name. My name became part of the song. It was a way to say thanks. I looked around. People were smiling at me. I danced proudly. I didn't usually dance. I didn't like people looking at me. But now I listened to the drum beating and let it guide my feet. I wished with all my strength for my mother to be watching and to feel proud of me. As I danced, I noticed a young Kazaan man, standing outside the circle of dancers, staring at me. He was tall, strongly built, his hair in long braids. His stare made me uncomfortable and I slid out of the circle of dancers and into the darkness again.

Things went well for many days, but then, slowly, in small ways, we all began to learn that in fact the people of Kazaan, although they had been kind to us, and fed us, and helped our children heal, and although their children and our children now ran and played and screamed and fought in the same way, were very different from us.

It was hard, at first, to understand this difference. My people had always been only with each other. We knew each other in the way we knew ourselves; we knew each other's habits and thoughts and behaviours. We became irritable and fought and made up again, but since we had to spend time both with those who made us happy and comfortable, and those who made us angry, it was important, when someone was angry, to be polite. I had always walked an awkward line, part of the clan and yet different. I had watched all my life as other people's friendships rose and shifted and changed, but never very much. After all, we were stuck with each other.

It had been the deepest division and sorrow any of us had ever known when our people had split because of arguing about how to manage when our old land had turned dry. Some of our people had gone south, and the rest of us had gone north, but the larger part of our people had stayed together. Many of the people who had left belonged to one family, and their leaving, while sad, hadn't destroyed our unity as a group.

Among our people, if someone had something, and someone else needed, they asked and it was given. Hides or tents or ropes or food or help; it was all shared. It flowed through the camp like a kind of river. Someone could always give the last of their food away, knowing that it would soon come back to them from someone else. We had always lived this way. It enabled us to live well, and it enabled us to all get along.

But the people of Kazaan were not like us. It was a painted clay bowl that showed us this difference.

I liked the bowl. I admired it. One day, I used it to bring some milk to Lani's tent. Other people admired it as well, and in the way of such things, over the next few days, the bowl went from hand to hand and tent to tent, it appeared and disappeared, sometimes it had food in it, sometimes it was sitting in a corner, sometimes a dog was licking scraps from it. And then one day, it slid from someone's hand and broke.

What I hadn't known is that the disappearance of the bowl was an event of some significance to the Kazaan.

Finally, one day, a whole group of women came to our tents. The woman who was in the front of the group was a very large woman named Botha. I had rather admired her largeness when I first saw her. I had never seen anyone before who was actually fat. I was amazed. I didn't know people could be fat. She was beautiful in her largeness. Now her chins quivered and shook. She held out her hand and pointed it at me. "Thief," she called me in their language. "Where is my bowl?"

I had no idea what she meant by thief. Our language had no word like this. But I understood that she needed the bowl, perhaps to put milk in, or something else.

I shook my head. "Broken," I said, in their language. "Gone."

"Thief," she roared at me again. I didn't understand the word. I heard the anger and accusation in her voice. I just had no idea what it was about.

I looked at Shuz, who had come up behind the group of women. She moved forward. "The bowl was…good," she said, using words I could understand.

I was still puzzled. Yes, the bowl was good, but it was just a bowl and now it was broken, someone would make another one. There were lots of bowls. They were easy to make.

The Kazaan women began to move through our camp, going in and out of the tents. A pile of things began to grow in the center of the camp, blankets and bowls and sticks and ropes.

Botha stormed back to me. "Mine," she said, pointing at the things. "Ours."

I still had no idea what she meant but I was very tired of being yelled at. I turned and stalked from the camp. I picked a bow, a blanket and a digging stick from the pile as I went.

I heard the women yelling behind me but I paid no attention.

But later that night, Lani and I talked it over. It was clear to us that the people of Kazaan had a strange attachment to bowls and blankets and digging sticks, as if they were children or mothers or lovers. We tried to understand it. We were the strangers here. But no matter how many ways we turned this idea over and examined it, it made no sense.

"Imagine saying to a tree or a dog, come here, you are mine," Lani giggled. "As if a tree or a dog would notice. How foolish you would look, calling such things to listen."

I put my chin in my hands. "Black Horse was mine, perhaps," I said. "I thought he was my family. But then he met another family he liked better."

"I can see liking a bowl, or a blanket, especially when it took a long time to make. I can see getting used to it. It is wonderful to come home at night, to a tent and a bed and furs, to comfort and the familiar," Lani mused. "But if you were hungry, would it feed you? If you were lonely, is a blanket or a bowl any comfort? Only sharing with each other can do that."

"But there's something more," Lani continued after a pause for thought. "How can that big woman, Botha, say come here, go there, to the other women? I watched their faces. She made them come into our tents and take things. They didn't want to do it. How does that connect to a broken bowl?"

"And Shuz does so much work for her, and yet never goes into the big woman's house," I said. We sighed together, mystified by it all.

Then Lani laughed. "When you left, the woman puffed up like a male grouse in spring. But she didn't dance, only yelled."

I laughed too. It was a good picture. I could see it. But it was also clear that our time with the Kazaans was coming to a close, and it would soon be time to move on.

But we had no real wish to move on yet. And Lani was in no shape to travel. Her baby was due.

The next night, a day after the visit of the Kazaan women to our camp, I heard her cry out. When I got to her tent, she was standing, holding on to the tent pole with one hand, the other on her belly. I built up her fire and called the elder women. That morning, just as the sun was rising, red as fire, Lani's new baby slid, wet and squalling, into the world. I was sitting beside her and she put this new person, a baby girl, into my arms. The baby opened its black eyes and looked up at me.

"I will look after you," I whispered. "I will keep you safe."

The next day, while Lani was still recovering, I went out with Shuz. She had undertaken a new task, cutting grass and piling it to dry.

"Why?" I asked, pointing at the grass. Many other Kazaans were also out on the plain, cutting grass.

"Winter is coming," she said. "Snow, cold, no food."

I had seen snow once or twice in my life, but in our old land, it came rarely and didn't last. Now, I learned from Shuz that a season was coming when no one should be abroad on these vast plains. That night, I came to the council fire, and I told the people this, although not everyone believed me. When we lived in the south, they were used to a rainy season with only a few days of snow and ice that soon passed.

Shuz had told me that in her land, the snow and ice lasted for much longer, many, many days, that the wind came howling over the flat land like a giant wildcat with teeth, and that we must prepare ourselves, must store food and warm sleeping robes, must patch our worn tents and make ourselves new clothes and footwear.

And she also made it clear the Kazaans didn't want to help us anymore. They had given us what they could, she said, but they wanted to save the rest of what they had for themselves. And we had proved ourselves to be bad people, by taking their things and breaking them. If we wanted anything more, we would have to trade for it.

So we sat in our torn and tattered tents, ate our own food, and slowly grew bitter, a feeling that was new to most of us.

The men went hunting every day; every day I watched in dread in case they brought in a black horse carcass, but mostly they brought small game, rabbits and birds. It wasn't enough. If we were going to survive a period of long cold, we needed fat; we needed meat and lots of it. We needed hides and fur.

The women did what they could. They tanned rabbit hides and sewed them together to make robes. They even tanned the bird skins with the feathers left on. They patched tents with bits and pieces of worn leather. They dried what extra meat and berries they could find in the sun and stored them away. The children roamed the plains looking for wood for fires, and slowly our tents grew warm again, and there were two new babies born.

But it wasn't enough. We needed something to trade, something for which the people of Kazaan would give much, would give us fatty meat and milk and hides, the things we needed most, and of which they had plenty. We knew that. We had seen inside their houses. But what could we, who had so little, give them, who had so much? I turned this thought over and over in my mind and had no answer.

One night, a few days later, after the sheep were in the pen, and Shuz and I had taken leave of each other, I went past the fires of my people to where Lani was sitting, cross legged in the dust beside the fire, piecing together bits of hide for the children to wear on their feet when it got cold.

"We have to be able to trade," I said. I had been thinking about this all day. "We have to find something they want. I think I know what it is."

Lani said nothing except to glance at the baby sleeping on the hide next to her. It was a happy baby, smiling and waving its arms around; I never paid much attention to babies but I smiled and played with this one because it was part of Lani and she was part of me. It always felt like she was the one part of world that I would never be able to bear to lose. Somehow, she and my mother had become tangled up inside me.

She shifted position and put down her work. "And what are you thinking now?" she asked. "There is always a plan in your head somewhere."

"Before we came to the Kazaans, I was going to bring all the horses back to be our friends. I had a picture in my head of how it could be."

She stared at me. "You're going to give them horses," she said.

I nodded and stared into the golden heart of the fire. Lani always knew my thoughts.

"I have been watching and learning from Shuz. I understand now what she does, how the sheep go where they go and why they stay in a pen to be killed instead of running away. I have learned much from her. Now I understand why, when I was last with the horses, they let me stay, they let me sleep in their company, they stopped running away. They had let me in to be part of their clan."

"Yes, but how can you get them to come here? When they see so many strange people, and the stinky Kazaans with their big houses, they will run away again. No matter if you are their friend."

"No, I have another idea. First, I am going to ask these Kazaans for salt."

"Salt?"

"These people have salt. They give it to their sheep and goats. They get it somewhere. I can get some—somehow. The horses will get used to coming to me for salt. I will build a pen and put the salt inside until they are used to the pen. Then I will make a gate and close the pen."

"And the black horse?"

"I will bring him here to live with us, he and some of his friends. The rest we will use for food and to trade with these Kazaans. I will show them the secret of how we use the black horse to carry things and to ride on. I am sure they will want horses of their own when they see what I can do. But I hope they choke on such a trade."

I thought about Black Horse, how gentle he was, and proud and playful. Would the Kazaans care for horses the way I did or would they see them as tools, or just more food?

"Morven, you must not do this, you are my sister and my friend. This act will change you. It will hurt you too much."

"Lani, you didn't listen when I spoke in council as to what Shuz told me. It will get too cold to go out. The ground and water turn hard as stone. The wind blows over the plains like a knife cutting flesh. We must have food and fat and skins. Your child will need you to eat well so you can feed her."

She sighed. "We are all doing everything we can, Morven. We have had hard times before. We will survive. Do not do this thing."

I stood and left. I stalked through the camp, went past the firelight, out to the edge of the camp, where I could look back. I could see light through the skins of tents of my people, but the log and skin huts of the Kazaans were dark. A child cried. Someone was singing and someone laughed. I turned and went out farther. Spotted Dog was at my heels. I found the place where the dogs curled together and I came among them, curled up with them. But their bodies against me gave me only warmth without comfort. I lay awake in the darkness, my mind busy, planning.

The next day, I asked Shuz for salt. Late that afternoon, after the sheep were penned, she took me to the elders. By now I had enough of the language to talk to them but I still didn't understand them. I asked them for salt. All my life I had been used to asking for what I wanted and needed and if someone had it, they gave and if they didn't, I asked somewhere else. The circle of elders was made up of old men and old women including the two I had first met when I came into the camp. They listened to me without comment. Shuz helped when I ran out of words.

"What will you give for it?" asked one old man. His eyes were almost shut and he had a few straggly hairs hanging from his chin and his head. I was puzzled. I looked at Shuz. She shrugged.

"What do you give?" he said again, impatiently. "You must trade something for the salt. Not free."

"Meat," I said. "Horses, meat, skins, fat."

They all looked at me. One of the old women leaned over and said something in the man's ear.

He waved his hand at me. "Go away," he said. "You make foolish promises. We have hunters, they bring meat and hides. You have nothing. You will give us nothing. Go away."

My mouth fell open and I closed it again. I had no words. There were no words in my head to fall out of my mouth. I wasn't used to not being believed. My people might think I was strange but by now, they believed what I told them.

Shuz touched my arm lightly and then rose and went outside. I followed her.

"Shuz, I need salt. I am going to catch horses. You can come, you will see, I can do it."

She looked at me. She had strange eyes, a sort of greeny-blue. It was often hard to tell what she was looking at since she never looked at me directly but looked over my shoulder or at the ground. Now she pulled her hair over her eyes and turned away. I watched her walk. There was something strange in her walk. Then I saw her hand, trailing at her side, her fingers moving, making signs. I followed. She ducked into one of the houses where I had never been. I followed her inside. It was dark inside; I could barely make out her shape in the gloom. She went to the back, lifted a pile of hides, pulled out a block of something wrapped in another hide.

"For the sheep," she said, and went back out.

I understood. Of course, she could take salt to the sheep and no one would question where it went. I followed again. She took the package of salt to the pen where the sheep were and scattered some of it on the ground. Then she rewrapped the rest and put it down beside the rock wall. She walked away without looking at me.

It took me a few days to make my preparations. I told only Lani and Dura my plans. I left early one morning. I thought that after we had left, the horses would have gone back to the bowl-shaped valley where we had first seen them. But we had left that place many days behind on our journey. I climbed up out of the valley where the village of Kazaan lay, up onto the high flat plains, cut here and there by deep gorges full of trees and tall grass. The horses could be in any one of these.

That night, I curled against Spotted Dog on a mat of tall grass that I had bent over and made into a soft nest. The sky blazed bright with stars; bands of light roved and waved over it. I could hear voices on the wind and in the grass. I thought perhaps my mother was speaking to me but I couldn't be sure. I often wondered about death but it didn't make any sense to me. I had watched so many animals and people die. They were there, and then they were gone. Where had my mother gone? Was she close, watching me? I wanted to talk to her. I wanted to hear her voice. The shaman had said she was watching. What had he meant? Was she close or was she far away? What was this other world like?

"Ma," I said out loud but only the wind answered. And then an owl. Or perhaps it was her? How could I know?

The night was cold. I had brought a skin with me but it was old and thin. I didn't make a fire because there was only grass to burn. Eventually, I slept.

I travelled the next day and the day after that. Gradually, the flat plain changed into a land of rolling hills, with trees and brush lining the ravines between each hill. Then I saw signs of the horses' presence: dung, grass that had been cropped. I began to track them. I came upon them on the fifth day, where I expected to find them, near where Black Horse had run away, in the centre of a bowl shaped valley, grazing slowly along a creek, under a fringe of enormous trees. They remembered me and didn't run although they snorted and threw up their heads. I came among them with handfuls of salt, and although they were hesitant at first, eventually, they licked my hands and blew and snorted and went back to grazing.

Black Horse was there. He had grown taller and his neck had thickened. He rubbed his head against my hair and pushed at me to get more salt. When I went to make camp, he followed. He and the spotted dog sniffed noses, and that night, while I slept, he stood over me.

He was gone in the morning when I woke, but not far. I spent the day wandering with them, and that night I made a fire, cooked some fish and berries together. I put salt on the fish after it was cooked and ate too much of it because I had craved salt for so long.

I had already spotted the place to build the pen. Dura arrived several days later. He had tracked me as I asked. I had told him to give me time to get reacquainted with the horses and to then come and help me. I wanted Dura because he already knew Black Horse, and because he was a hard worker who wouldn't ask too many questions. We had made a plan, but of course it depended on how quickly I found the horses. I was glad to see him. Now I showed him how to behave among the new horses. It was hard for him, he was a hunter, but he listened to me and he wanted to learn. The horses ran from him at first, but because Black Horse knew him, that helped to build trust with the others. Every morning, I made him come with me to take salt to them, and, in the afternoon, to help me to cut the tall grass that grew along the creek and pile it in the space I had picked for the pen.

One afternoon, as we were taking a break, he said quietly, "The horses trust you. They are gentle. I understand now, why you care for them. You are like them, Morven, strong but gentle."

I had no idea what to say to this. After a while, I said, "With the horses, I feel as if I belong. I know how to behave. I understand them. People are harder to understand. It has always been that way with me. Being with animals is where I am comfortable, where I understand what to do."

"And yet many of your people admire you."

"They do?"

"And Luz has told us that you have brought the people a great gift, that horses will change all our lives."

I thought about this. Then I said bitterly, "I wanted to be with the horses because I was curious about them. Then I learned their ways and I understood that they were both powerful and gentle. And now I am preparing to betray them for the sake of our people. Every day, while we prepare, I feel sick with the knowledge of what I am doing. And yet it will give Black Horse and his friends back to me. Is this a good thing? Why should I be admired for this?'

"It is not wrong to care for both people and horses."

"Let's just work and not talk."

We also had to cut trees and pile up stones to make the pen. Cutting whole trees with stone axes was very hard work. The blades got dull quickly, and we had to search for the right kind of stone to make new ones. Dura and I sweated and grunted with effort in the afternoon sun. But the evenings were cold and getting colder and at night, we huddled close to the fire, wrapped in our thin robes with no tent. We worked all day and then we still had to take time to hunt for food. Luckily, there was fish in the stream, and Spotted Dog helped by bringing in small animals. The berries were gone from the bushes and the leaves on the trees were turning brown and falling to the ground.

One morning when we woke, the sky was gray, and an icy wind was blowing in our faces. We warmed up as we worked, but not much. By afternoon, it had started to snow. We worked on but our hands and feet finally grew too numb to hold the axe handles, and we retreated to the fire. Dura went in search of dry wood. The horses were ensconced in the thick brush beside the river; Dura and I needed shelter. We couldn't spend the night in the wind and the snow.

Finally, we retreated to the shelter of a large, broad branched tree, where we huddled together against the trunk, dozing while the wind shook the tree above us. I was conscious of Dura's warmth, of his musky male smell. I wasn't attracted to him but we were spending all our time together and sometimes at night, after I had rolled myself into my furs, he would sit across the fire and watch me. I tried to ignore him. Mostly we worked. I turned away his efforts to make conversation. I didn't want to think too much about Lani, or what I was doing or why. The next day, we took enough time to build a shelter. I was worried. The snow must mean that the cold of which Shuz had spoken would soon be upon us.

But I was wrong. The next day, the sun came back full of heat, and the snow was soon gone. I knew it would return. We worked until dark, fell into bed and worked again and again, day after day and then, finally, it was done.

The horses had gotten used to going in the pen every day for grass and salt. At first they didn't notice that we had closed the gate; when they did, they panicked. They plunged around and around the pen in despair but they never challenged the fence. This was something that had worried me, that they would look at our puny fence and simply crash their way through it. But they didn't. Eventually, they settled enough to eat the grass we brought them. Every once in a while, one of them would panic all over again and they would all run for a while. Each time, they calmed faster.

In the morning they were still there. We went among them with grass and water and salt. They were hungry and glad to see us. I brought a rope with me and put it around Black Horse and took him out of the pen. Then I took red ochre paint, and marked the shoulders of the horses that would live: mares and their babies. The others, the young males, and some of the older females, would die.

I left Dura there to keep cutting grass and carrying water. I got on Black Horse and after a lot of arguing, persuaded him to leave and go towards the village of Kazaan. Once we were out of sight of his family, we travelled fast together. On the evening of the third day, we rode into Kazaan.

The people came out of their houses and watched us in silence. I rode past their houses and towards the tents of my people. Behind me, I could hear muttered conversation that grew to a buzz and then even louder. I didn't look behind; I could hear their footsteps.

We went through the tents of my people until we reached Lani's tent. The children came pouring out and greeted Black Horse like a long lost member of the family. They swung on his tail and slid off his back and he put his head down and blew horse breath in their hair. I saw the hunters looking at me and I called them to come. I described what I had done, where the horses were, and what I wanted them to do. They ran excitedly, gathered their bows and spears and bone knives, packed some food and sleeping skins, and left.

But the Kazaan hunters were no fools. They noticed the men leaving. They looked at each other, torn between their desire to watch me and Black Horse and their desire to find out where the hunters were going.

In the end, their hunting instinct won and they turned and left. The women crowded forward, staring at me. Shuz was the first to come forward. She bent her head towards Black Horse, as she would do for any strange animal and he blew on her. She held out her hand and he licked it. She turned towards me. It was the first time I had seen her face full of joy instead of sadness.

I stood beside her and showed her how to scratch Black Horse in his favourite places. "You…you…" she gestured towards his back and then looked at me, puzzled.

I nodded. I didn't really have a word for it either. "He carries me," I said. "Together, we can go far and fast, farther and faster than before. Sometimes he carries the children, or the tents."

She walked all around him, her face thoughtful. Then she looked a question at me. I nodded. She swung her leg over his back and sat there. I took the rope and led him in a circle. All the women and children followed in a mass, which made him nervous.

"Stay back," I snapped and they hung back a little.

When I stopped, Shuz slid down. Her face was alight in a curious way. She looked at me. "This is..." She gestured, struggling for the word. "It is…like the sheep, but better. This is a great thing. You have brought us a great thing."

She walked away and I saw her bend her head toward the other Kazaan women, who hurried towards her. Then they all went off in a chattering clump. It was odd to see Shuz surrounded by women. Since I had known her, she seemed to spend most of her time alone. It was one of the reasons I had chosen to spend time with her. I had noticed that both the women and the men ignored her, unless they needed her to do something. Then they spoke to her in an odd tone, one with an edge to it. She always startled when she heard someone speak to her; she hurried around with her head down and her hair over her face. She had a blanket woven from the hair of the sheep that she wore around her shoulders, and she often pulled it up to cover her face. I didn't understand why she did this, and I didn't have the language to ask her about it.

I tied Black Horse near the tent so he could eat grass and not run away. Lani brought food. The children pulled my hair and flopped into my lap and then ran away screaming with laughter.

"The men should be back in many days with food and skins," I said.

She reached over and took my hand. "You have done a great service for us all. We will eat and be warm through this cold time you say is coming."

I took my hand back. For some reason, my throat hurt and I was angry. "I must go back," I said. "The females and their babies will be frightened. I want to bring them here. I want them to be part of our tribe."

Lani sighed. "You must rest first," she said.

"I can rest while you and the Kazaans eat my friends," I said.

"Oh, Morven, you are never satisfied. You always want so much. You always want things to be different than they are. You are so restless inside, like something wild lives inside you. You come and then you go and you never sit at my fire, with your sisters, in peace."

I heard her words and the reproach in them. I knew she carried too many burdens, too many mouths to feed, too much worrying about how we would go there or do this. In the mornings, Lani was the one the other women turned to for ideas of where to go, what to do, where to look for food, what needed doing in the camp.

"And what will you do for food for him and his family," she gestured at Black Horse, "when this cold and these winds come that you talk about."

I had no answer. I had wondered that myself. I had already asked Shuz. She showed me the piles of cut grass they had stored for the sheep, but I could never cut enough grass to feed all the horses. But if the women and men all helped me, perhaps it could be done. But would the men help?

I looked at Black Horse, now just a shadow at the edge of the firelight. I could take him back and turn him loose. He would be the leader now; he would be the only male left. The mares and their babies would be in his care. He was a lot of trouble. Even I didn't understand why I went to such an effort. Lani was right. Why did I always want to change everything?

I heard voices and both Lani and I turned to look. Shuz and some other women stepped from the darkness. They were carrying bundles that they laid beside the fire. There were skins, bundles of dried fat and meat mixed with berries and a bag of salt. Shuz looked at me. "This is their trade," she said. "They want you to teach them," she said. "They want to know how...how he carries you, how he listens to you. We don't understand. You will teach us all."

I looked at them. I looked at the food, enough for many weeks, enough to keep Lani and her child and the rest of the clan, warm and fed. Lani smiled at me but I turned my head away. I had done what I had done for the people, but really, most of all, I had done it for Lani. I was angry at myself for betraying the horses, and now, to avoid facing it, I focused this anger on her.

"Yes," I said to Shuz. "I will teach you. I will teach all of you, both my clan and yours."

I stood up and stalked off through the darkness to my own tent.

Chapter Eight

I slid out of my tent and stood stretching in the sun. There was heat in the sun and green blades of grass shoving through the mud. It had been a long winter but this day was warm, the sky blue. Birds swooped and twisted in the sky, which was a deep blue.

Shuz hadn't exaggerated. The cold winds had come not long after we had managed to get all of the mares and their children back to Kazaan. We had made a pen for them and we had cut as much long grass as we could but of course, it wasn't even close to enough. On days when the wind wasn't blowing and the sun shone, however cold it was, we took them with us and wandered in search of grass while they pawed at the snow and fed themselves.

Shuz had made friends with a small yellow mare and now rode with me. All the horses stayed calm around Shuz. She had a way of making small quiet noises under her breath; she moved easily and slowly among them. Very quickly, she had caught on to the ways I showed her of making the small mare move and stop. She even invented new ideas. We experimented with various ways to tie ropes and discovered that a series of ropes on their heads worked better than a rope around the neck.

I had my own tent, my own food that winter. I put my tent on the outside of the clan circle and I slept alone at night, with several dogs curled by my side and layers of skins and furs over me to keep me warm. I often lay awake, staring into the fire, while the winds shook the tent and snow blew over the flat land.

Lani looked at me with hurt eyes when I passed. I wasn't angry with her, but neither did I feel like talking—to her or to anyone else. Something had gone from me when I left the horses behind to their fate. When I thought about that day, it was like a black place opened inside me, a black place that stayed with me and kept separate from other people. I didn't want to see that black place and so it was easier to stay away from her.

But the people of Kazaan also saw what they wanted to see. All winter I would wake to find small gifts left outside my tent, cooked food, or once a string of polished black beads on a leather string, once a woven piece of cloth like the one Shuz wore, but this was made of many colours woven together. I put it on my bed. Then I hung it on the tent wall. Finally I took it down and put it away in its own bag.

They watched me as I walked through their places; they stepped aside for me. There were usually two or three people watching as Shuz and I took the horses and the sheep and goats out to graze.

Shuz saw nothing. Her life was the animals. We had enough language now to talk to one another. One day we were sitting huddled together for warmth under a small tree, watching the horses and the sheep desperately working away, pawing at the snow, burying their noses in the snow to find the grass underneath. The sheep followed the horses, sometimes almost underneath them, eating the grass as fast as the horses could uncover it.

"Which house here is your family?" I said. I hadn't been able to work it out. As far as I could tell, Shuz mainly slept in the same pen as the sheep or sometimes she slept with the dogs. She got food from various houses.

"These people are not my family," she said. I heard a sharp edge in her voice that I had never heard before. Usually she kept her voice soft; often I had to push my head close to hers in order to hear.

"My family are gone," she said. "They were hungry and the people of Kazaan gave them some food and sent them away. I was hurt and couldn't walk. My family left me. These Kazaans kept me to work for them in trade for the food."

I opened my mouth and closed it again.

"Someday I will find my own people," said Shuz. "Someday I will leave this place. I am not of these people or of this place."

This was a new thought and I had to work at it to understand. I had never heard of someone without a family. It couldn't be done. You were whatever family you were born to, you had a mother and sisters and brothers and your mother's relatives were your relatives. I had never met someone who was alone. I shook my head. "But how do you live?" I said finally.

"The animals are my family. The sheep, and now, the horses. And the dogs, sometimes. I care for them and the Kazaans give me food."

"Dura was not born of our people," I said. "But when he joined us, because he came with me, he became part of my uncle and my mother's family. He didn't want to go back to his people. He wanted to stay with us, but he needed a family. How would he live, otherwise?"

Shuz only shook her head and pulled her hair over her face.

We were silent all the rest of the day. But that night, as we slid onto the horses in order to lead the rest of them home, she said, abruptly, "Perhaps you could be my family. Perhaps you could be my sister."

And then she turned her head away and made the mare go fast away from me and we didn't talk of it again. I thought of Lani and how she had been like my sister, once. These days I avoided her and my own little sisters. Seeing them only made me feel guilty for neglecting them.

Now I stood outside my tent, enjoying the heat in the sun. The wind smelled sweet. I had been putting off teaching the Kazaans to ride, making excuses; it had been too cold, I said, or there was too much snow, I had to feed the animals. But now those excuses were gone and so was the snow. Every day the horses rolled and rolled to get the mats of dead hair off themselves. They crowded towards me every morning now when I came to fetch them, eager to get to the new grass out on the plains.

This morning I picked one of the younger mares to work with. Shuz and I had spent all winter getting all the horses used to the idea of ropes. This one was quiet and friendly. I spent some time with a wooden comb taking the dust and mud and dead hair off her brown back. She stretched and shook herself and a cloud of dust rose into the air. Finally, I turned and beckoned in the general direction of the group of young men who stood nearby.

They seemed to be always nearby, these young men, when I was working with the horses. They were both fascinated and frightened. At first they had crowded in too close and I had snapped at them to back away. Now they followed at the distance, watching Shuz and I with sullen faces and narrow eyes. I had caught them a couple of times in the pen with the horses and warned them away.

"I will teach you when I am ready," I had told them. And, to be fair, they had waited, although not patiently.

One of the young men now slouched towards me, half pleased and half afraid, looking back at the others and then at me. "I am Kai," he said, and looked over his shoulder to be sure everyone was watching him. He was the same man who had stared at me during the dancing. I had noticed his eyes on me at other times.

I showed him how to greet the mare, how to comb her, scratch her, placate her. I thought he was paying attention but when I turned to put the comb away, and before I could stop him, he had jumped on her back. He sat there for half a moment, before the mare reared back, broke the thin rope holding her to the fence, and took off across the prairie jumping and kicking. He fell off almost immediately and lay there stunned, then sat up. The assembled onlookers were laughing so hard they were bent over and holding on to one another.

I turned on them in fury. "Go away," I yelled. "Go away, go home to your mothers. You are like babies. If you want me to teach you, learn to pay attention." I stomped off across the grass, first to Kai, who wasn't hurt, but wouldn't look at me, and then in search of the escaped mare.

I spent the next few days with her, getting her used to me, getting her used to my weight, used to the rope, my voice. She was like a child I was teaching. Every day I brought her a bit of salt. I made Kai stand beside me and do what I was doing. He was like another child, but it was clear he was a leader among the young men. If I could teach him, he would be able to pass on my lessons to the others.

Finally, many days later, I beckoned to him again. I motioned to him to get on the horse. He looked a question at me and I nodded. He swung his leg up and sat on the mare. This time the horse stood still; she was used to Kai and to me and trusted us. This time, we walked around together until they both started to relax.

The next day, we went riding together, Kai on the brown mare and myself on the black horse. We rode side by side over the plain, over the new grass, with the giant blue bowl of sky over our heads and birds tumbling and playing with each other. Kai's face was often twisted in pain; he hadn't realized that riding a horse involved bouncing up and down on a bony back. After that, we went riding every day. I tied a thick leather pad over the mare's back and that helped him.

By the end of many hands of days, the young men and women who were interested were matched to various horses. We all began going on rides together; despite their sore legs and bums, when they came back, the young men, led by Kai, swaggered through the camp. The men who rode began eating together around a separate fire. I heard from Shuz that they had a new name for themselves: the horsemen.

Shuz and I laughed when we heard this. "Then we are the sheep women, the goat women, the dogs, the horses. We are all of these."

It was a fine summer, just the same. There were many new foals. Black Horse was the stallion now, and many of the new horses looked like him. There were baby sheep, bouncy baby goats, and new human babies. There was much to eat and the sun shone every day. We rode, we hunted, we found more wild horses and brought them into the camp. By now, every family had someone who was getting used to horses. Some of the older quieter mares I taught to carry burdens, noisy children, sacks and water jugs. My people and the people of Kazaan were beginning to intermingle. Babies were born that had the look of Kazaans. Lani was pregnant again. Dura was often at her fire or spent his nights with her.

One day I watched a group of young men from our clan ride out onto the plains. When they came back that night, they had killed several large deer. They had fresh meat and hides hanging on the backs of the horses. The women whooped and laughed as the men rode into camp.

That night, around the fire, the men told stories of the successful hunt. I stayed in my tent but I could still hear the laughter, singing and drumming.

Another night, when I went by on the way to my own tent, I noticed a circle of people at Lani's fire. Some were people of Kazaan, some were our own people. Someone was singing, several people had drums. Even two of the elders were there. For a moment I stopped. I watched them sing and laugh while I stood in the darkness. Then I passed by. Though Lani often looked at me, we said little to each other.

That night, after I went to my tent, someone scratched at the outside. Spotted Dog barked and growled. I crawled back outside and stood up. Kai was standing there, shifting from foot to foot, looking foolish.

"I brought you this," he said. He held out a carved wooden comb. The wood had been inlaid with bits of bone and blue stones to make a pattern. It was beautiful. I knew what it was. It was a courting gift, the kind of gift a man gave a woman when he wanted to spend the night in her tent, the kind of gift that Dura had given Lani when he first came to our clan.

I turned it over. I did like pretty things, and by now, thanks to the people of Kazaan, I had quite a lot of them. I handed it back.

"No," I said. I turned to go back in the tent and Kai grabbed my arm.

"I want to stay with you," he said. "I am coming in."

I looked at his hand on my arm. Among our people, when a woman says no, that is an end to it. Sometimes she says no for a while, sometimes she says yes, right away.

Sometimes a man brings her many gifts; sometimes no gifts are needed.

I lifted his hand off my arm. I had no wish to be like Lani, surrounded by children, always either pregnant or nursing. I could welcome Kai into my tent and probably no child would come, because I didn't wish for a child. But neither did I want to spend my nights with Kai or any other man. I had never wanted this, had never felt the urges the other women talked about and giggled about at night that compelled them to the sleeping robes with a man.

Lani and I had talked about this. After Dura had spent the night, her face always had a soft, satisfied look. "It is a good thing," she said to me. "Why don't you want it?" I had no explanation for her. It seemed such an intrusion, to let someone else, another body, into my tent, my bed, my life.

"No," I said again, more forcefully. "Go from here, Kai, I am not for you."

"But you are for me," he said. "I wish it. I wish to stay."

He grabbed me again, both arms this time, pulled me towards him, tried to turn me around and shove me towards the door of the tent. Instead, I stepped backwards, brought my foot down on the middle of his foot, banged my head backwards so that the back of my head slammed into his nose, then spun around, grabbed his arm and threw him on the ground. He landed heavily, yelling in pain. Spotted Dog stood over him, growling and ready to bite.

"Go now, "I said. I grabbed the dog and pulled him away. Kai stood up and limped away without another word.

When I saw him the next morning, he turned his face away. His nose was swollen and he was limping. We never rode together again. He rode with the other men and sometimes with the young women but he avoided me.

The rest of the summer went quickly, there was much to do. Now that I knew what to expect for the next winter, I set our people to cutting and drying grass. But there was always something else that needed to be done as well, berries to pick and dry, wood to gather. The people of Kazaan gathered white clay mud from a particular place near the creek, and from this they made many things, water jugs and bowls, but also, decorations for people and houses which they painted. They made colours from berries and leaves and red rocks, and they made clothes from skins of animals they killed as well as the wool and hair from the sheep and goats.

Life was as peaceful and easy as it had ever been. Shuz had made a small tent for herself and pitched it next to mine. We spent evenings together in my tent, lying on the sleeping robes, staring into the fire.

One night, she said, "I heard the elders talking about you. Kai has told them you are a bad person. He says you hate men, that you tried to kill him by getting the horse to throw him on the ground. The elders say, yes, you are dangerous. They think you will be a shaman some day. They say you have too much power. They say you and your people are dangerous."

I sat up. "I have no power and I don't wish for any. Kai fell off because he is a fool. But now he rides with the others. Everyone is happy. Our children play together. The men hunt together. We share the horses."

She shrugged. "They say you are a seer, that you know too much and see too much. They think you should go."

I stared at her. "How can they make me go or stay? I do what I please."

"They say this is their land, and someday you will try to take it from them."

I could only shake my head. None of this made sense.

After Shuz left, I sat for a long time over the dying embers of the fire. I remembered the strange visions I had when I first came to Kazaan and sat in the elders' tent.

After a while, sitting there, I began to dream. At least it felt like a dream. I had left the tent and was flying over the land. It was dark outside but I was flying towards a reddish light, like the light of the sun rising over the land.

As I came towards the sun, I realized how far I could see. The land was shining bright, green and blue where small lakes and rivers lay in the folds and hollows of the land. It was like a beautiful woven blanket. There were herds of animals, horses, deer, bison. Everywhere life ran and flew and hopped and played on the land. I flew farther and farther; the land changed and now I was flying over ice and snow. Below me were different animals, giant white bears and huge fish in the water and enormous flocks of birds.

I flew on and now I was flying over an immense forest, trees reaching far up into the sky, an endless expanse of trees, and very few animals except small creatures that chattered and hid. And ahead a range of mountains, glistening white and blue. As I came towards them I realized I might not be able to fly over them; I tried to go higher and higher, I pushed my aching body and aching breath up, up, up; it got colder and colder and still all that was beneath me was long slopes of ice and snow, and then just when I thought I couldn't go any further and might have to turn back, I saw a gap between two mountain peaks. I arrowed towards it, shot through and slid down a long slope of air, and then abruptly awoke beside my dying fire, confused and slightly afraid.

What had just happened? The dream had seemed so real. What had Shuz said, that the Kazaan elders thought I was a seer? What did that mean? Is that what this dream had been? Could I really see places that were far away? It had been a dream but it also felt real.

I crawled into my sleeping robes but it took me a long, long time to fall asleep.

In the morning, when I arrived at the pen where the horses were kept at night, two men of Kazaan were standing at the gate. I ignored them and went to go past them, open the gate and take the horses out to graze and drink.

They stepped in front of me.

"Go away," they shouted at me. "These are not your horses. These belong to Kazaans. Go away."

The words came into my head and swirled around like water. They made no meaning, although now at least I had some idea of what belonging meant to the Kazaans. I moved again to go past the men and this time, when they stepped in front of me, they held sticks above their heads, ready to swing them at me.

I backed away until I was out of range.

"Men of Kazaan," I said, "the horses belong to everyone. But right now they need food and water. We can figure this out later. We will sit and talk it over."

"Go away," they said again. That was their only response, that, and the sticks.

I turned and went in search of Shuz. I couldn't find her. As I walked through their camp, the people of Kazaan turned their faces away from me. What was going on? This made no sense. Until today, things had been peaceful.

Lani might know, I thought.

And Lani did. I had never seen her like this. She was standing outside the tent with her baby on her hip. "What have you done?" she asked.

It was a morning for strange comments and questions.

I shrugged. "There are men at the horse pen waving sticks at me."

"They want us to leave, these people, these Kazaans. A group of women came this morning, early. It was that big woman with all the chins, and her friends. They said we must all go. They said we can only take what we came with. Nothing more. They said this place belongs to them and that we can no longer belong here. How can that be? What do they mean?"

"And what has this to do with me?"

"I don't know. They mentioned you. They called you 'the red-headed one.' They said because of you, we must all go. They said you are trying to kill their young men."

We stared at each other.

"It is something to do with the horses," I said slowly. "They have this idea of belonging. It is a strange idea but it seems to matter. They say mine, yours. They think even people can belong to them or not. Shuz has no family here. No one will take her in because she isn't part of their family even though she does their work for them."

"Then maybe it is time we did go," Lani said, suddenly, fiercely. "Why have we stayed so long? What are these people to us, or us to them? I haven't forgotten that except for you, we might have all died in the cold last winter."

"But they will want to keep the horses," I said. "All the horses."

"Let them. There are other horses."

"No," I said. "I will not. The horses come with me. They are my family."

Lani snorted, a sound somewhere between anger and laughter. "Your family. And what are we? Come through the camp with me and call everyone together. This must be decided right away."

"No. No one will want to leave. No one is ready. They will need time to think, to prepare, to pack." I hadn't expected Lani to react this way. Now when I looked at her face, I could see fury there. Perhaps she had been already thinking about leaving and this new move by the Kazaans had pushed her to a decision.

"We can't stay near people who have no manners. These people don't know how to behave. They are silly. They are like foolish, crazy people who have no sense. Come on, Morven."

"But why should we leave? They say they own this place. Why would they say this? No one can say who should stay here and who should go. Perhaps it is just a few fools. Perhaps we should talk to their elders and see what is real and what is not."

Lani stopped. "Fine. Go talk to them. Go see what they say. Then we will call the people together and you can explain it all to them, Morven. Somehow you are at the centre of this, I don't understand how or why. Just as I don't understand how you could pass by my fire night after night, without any greeting for me or your sisters. You have seemed so angry and I have watched you avoiding your people. And now that there is trouble, you want me to speak, you come to me for help, you stand here staring at me, making suggestions for what I ought to do."

She turned her back on me and stomped away. I stared after her, astonished. Had everything changed in the middle of the night while I was asleep, and now everyone was different from whom they had been? The horses, the men of Kazaan, Lani? What more could go wrong?

I went away myself to find the elders of Kazaan, and see if they could help me make sense of this new world. All I knew was what Shuz had reported. I needed to hear it for myself.

When I ducked through the low door of the elder's hut, the group of elderly men and women sitting there all stopped talking and stared at me. They were in a circle around a fire, wrapped in blankets, drinking hot water from clay cups, and passing a smoking pipe from hand to hand.

I sat on the ground by the fire and waited. Finally one of them, the old woman, sighed. "You are not welcome here," she said. "You have brought trouble into the world. You and your people must go before you bring more trouble."

"What trouble?" I asked angrily. "I have been your friend. I have helped with your animals. I have learned your language. I taught your people about horses. You said you wanted a trade. I have kept my part. Am I the one making trouble? It is not me, it is your young men that are the problem."

Now the old woman looked at me.

"We know what you have done," she said. "We have seen it in our dreams. But you don't know. You see, but not enough. You have broken the world open, you have brought new dreams into the world, you have made the young men excited and crazy, and now they must do something with such excitement. Now they are taller and faster than they have ever been. Now they want to do something with this new strength. They are bored. There is enough food. They don't need to go hunting. They are talking of travel, or going to see what the rest of the world looks like. They fight among themselves. This…" she shook her head, "this is what you have done. You have brought trouble, and pain and sorrow."

I opened my mouth and closed it again. What could I say?

Finally I said, "Then I will go and take the horses with me. Your young men should dream their own dreams. They don't need me for that."

The old woman laughed, an odd high-pitched sound.

"Dreams can never be undreamt. The horses will stay."

"But…"

"Go. Take your people and go from here before you break our world even farther." She turned her face away and stared into the fire. They all turned their eyes away and dismissed me.

I stood, and left. Outside I took deep breaths of the clean air after the smoky dark hut. I was shaking with anger. I thought of the men waving their stupid sticks. Anyone could wave a stick. Anyone could sharpen a stick or tie on a sharpened stone to make a spear. Anyone could do this. The young men of my people had been riding horses as well. They had gone on several more hunting trips with the horses and come back loaded with food, happy, shouting their triumph. They had shared out the meat as they always did. They had told stories around the fire of their adventures. So what had that old woman meant, that I had broken the world? I had made their stupid world better. I had given them a gift of the thing I loved, the gift of horses and riding. And this was the trade they gave me for it now?

A sudden image flashed into my mind. I was on the back of the black horse and the two men with sticks were on the ground. I would make Black Horse ride over top of them; I would smack my own stick onto their heads until they ran away in fear.

I had to talk to Lani. I hurried to her tent.

"You're right, we should go," I said as soon as I saw her. "Tell everyone to pack. We will find our own land, our own place, away from these strange people."

"What did the Kazaan elders say?"

"A lot of nonsense about things I didn't understand. And then they said we must go. And I agree with them. We have stayed too long with these people. I don't like them. I don't want to be near them anymore."

"Morven. Why have you changed? You said you wouldn't leave the horses."

"I won't." I paused. "I have been thinking, and I have a plan. I will come back at night for them. Let the Kazaans think we have gone away. Let them be the fools they are, and go sit around their fires inside thinking they made us afraid. Let them tell stories and sing songs to each other. The horses will go with us."

"But then the Kazaans might follow us."

"Let them. We will go far and fast."

"But we have children, food, tents to carry. We have been here a long time. The tents are full of things. It will take us quite a while to pack, to get organized."

"You are the one who said it was time to go. We will load everything on the horses. We will travel faster with them."

Lani shook her head. I could see she was thinking. She shook her head again. "No. I changed my mind. The people are not ready to go. They need to make their own decisions. We will hold a council and discuss this idea."

I went away from her. I was still angry. I was angry with everything. When Spotted Dog got in my way, I kicked him. He snarled at me and I was sorry but I didn't tell him so. Instead I went to my tent and began to take it down, to pack my things. But first I sat on my bed and looked at my tent and tried to think clearly.

I was still angry. I had rarely been so angry in my life. I had tried to avoid anger by avoiding people. I had felt sorrow when my mother died, and I had avoided Lani because she was someone I cared about. She knew too much about me, saw too clearly what I thought and felt.

I began to pack. There were a lot of things: the soft sheepskins from which I had made my bed, the beads that someone had left outside the tent, the new bow and knife I had finally had time to make.

By the time I had it all folded and wrapped and tied in a bundle. I realized it was far too heavy for me to carry. The black horse could carry it. I half carried it, half dragged it down the hill where Lani was sitting outside her tent. Some people were taking down their tents, but many were not.

I stood in front of Lani. "We must go now. You must persuade the people.""Morven, it is not my task to tell people what to do." Lani said. "The people are upset. Some have heard one thing, some another. Let us go together, talk to them, plan this move. Then we will all talk to the Kazaans. We can divide the horses. There is no need to be angry."

I sighed. Why was it all so complicated and slow? Why couldn't someone, me or Lani, just make a decision? Why all this endless talking?

But that night we met around the fire, and I outlined my plan: we would pack, and leave, or pretend to leave, but we would only go a little way, we would camp in a ravine to the west, and then I, and a group of young men, would come back for the horses.

"And do you think they won't notice that their precious horses are gone?" my uncle asked.

"What will they be able to do about it?" I asked.

Questions and discussion went furiously around the circle. Finally, Luz, the shaman, stood up and raised both arms and bent his head, asking for silence and attention. Everyone fell silent. He seldom spoke and when he did, his words were listened to carefully.

"You must listen to Morven," he said quietly. "She has a special place in this clan. She is one who goes ahead, she is one who sees what others do not. She has changed all our lives. Now we must leave this place, it is past time that we did. And we must take the horses. Follow Morven." He sat down and the people were quiet. Eventually, we all were exhausted but in basic agreement, and as the fire was burning low everyone went to their tents, some to sleep, some to keep arguing, some to pack.

The next morning, Lani looked at me, said nothing, then bent to the task of folding and wrapping bundles. Lani was making up smaller bundles for the older children to carry. But she had a new tent, bigger and heavier than the small travelling tents we were used to carrying.

"We have gotten soft," I said. "We have too many things, we have gotten used to easy food and easy warmth."

"What is wrong with easy food, warmth and comfort?' she snapped. "I never saw you turn it down."

I sighed. She bent and hoisted the tent to her back then let it drop. "Too heavy."

"Ask Dura to carry it."

"I could cut it, maybe, make it smaller. It could be two tents. We don't need one so big. I made it bigger than usual because of the children." She frowned and went back to her work.

By late afternoon, the clan had begun to straggle away from Kazaan in a ragged line. Our practiced ways of moving seemed to have been forgotten. All morning, there had been noisy quarrels among the people about what to carry, what to leave behind. Some, despite the speech from Luz, still didn't want to move. They didn't understand why we were leaving.

Several hunters had gone ahead to find the ravine I had told them about. I stood and watched as people left. There had been a lot of arguing all day but finally, everyone seemed ready. There had been a lot to pack. We had never stayed so long in one place before and we had accumulated too much.

The ravine was only half a day's walk away. I had taken the horses there sometimes in the winter, when the wind was too strong for them to stay out on the plain, and I knew there was water, grass and game. The people still grumbled as they walked, but in general I think most people were glad to be leaving Kazaan.

I watched everyone go and finally, I left myself. With some difficulty, I loaded my heavy tent, wrapped with all my stuff inside the tent roll, on my back, carried it over a hill, and then stashed it in a hollow, under trees and brush, out of sight. Then I circled around the long way until I could settle on a hill to the south where I could watch the Kazaans.

They had watched us leave but they hadn't let the horses out to graze so they were cutting grass and carrying it to them. Shuz and a couple of young girls were out with the sheep and goats. I needed to talk to Shuz and tell her what was going on so she could come with us if she wanted.

I sat there all afternoon, watched as they came in for the evening, as the evening fires were lit, as people went back and forth, fetching water and wood, as children came running for food. Gradually people went into their houses, the hides were pulled over doors, and the noise of singing or drumming fell away. The whole place went quiet and darkness fell on the village of Kazaan.

I found Shuz where she slept next to the sheep pen. "You know we have left. We are all meeting at that deep ravine west of here," I said. "If you want to come with us, pack your things and meet us there. Find Lani and her children. She will help you."

She nodded. "I have been watching you," she said. "I am ready to leave this place and these people. Can I also join your family?"

"Yes," I said. "But don't let anyone see you leave."

I left her there. I trusted her to say nothing and to find us. It was almost evening. I knew, as we had planned, that Dura and the other men would be waiting for me on the other side of the camp. But first, I had to make sure no one was watching the horses. I hadn't seen anyone with them, from my place on the hill but I wanted to be sure.

When it was dark, I slipped down the hill, trotted over the grass, and then slid quietly along the back of the houses, until I came to the horse pen. The horses, startled, moved uneasily, and then quieted when they realized it was me. I was over the fence and among the horses when I heard some men's voices.

"They're gone," one said. "Why do we have to be out here in the cold and the dark?"

"What if they come back? That one they call Morven, that red-headed one, she is full of tricks. I don't like the way they left, without a word, with no good-bye."

"They have no manners, those people. They don't know how to behave. Travelling around all the time. We don't know who they are or where they're from. It's good they have gone."

I moved among the horses, quietly. I found the black horse, slipped a rope around his nose and neck. He licked my hand, hoping for salt. The men were standing just beyond the gate. I could just see their silhouettes. Then I heard Dura's voice.

"Men of Kazaan," he said, quietly. "We have come to talk with you."

"What do you want?"

"We have come to take our share of the horses. We will leave some for you and take some for us. The women of our people need horses to carry tents and children. The men of our people have become used to having horses to go hunting with."

"No," said the men. "Go away, go back to your women. The horses are for us." Someone laughed. I thought perhaps it was Kai. I could hear, behind me, other men of my people, sliding quietly over the fence and moving, each one, to a horse. The horses were uneasy now and beginning to move around, but the other men were too busy arguing with Dura to notice. Other men were coming from the Kazaan houses. They wouldn't see very well in the dark after they had come out from the firelight.

I eased closer to the gate. Dura was doing a fine job of pleading our case, arguing, waving his arms. The other men were yelling now. Good.

It only took a second to slide the gate poles out of their sockets. The men's yelling covered any noise.

"Now," I yelled, and threw my leg over Black Horse's back, slid on, pulled him around and smacked him with the end of my rope. Hard. The men behind me did the same. The horses burst out of the gate. I pulled Black Horse so he ran directly at the two men. At the last moment, the man I was aiming for dodged, but I swung my stick at the other man and saw him fall.

I had been aiming at his shoulders but he ducked and I hit his head.

Then we were out and away. I heard a yell behind me. I thought it was Dura but I couldn't tell. I was hanging on as tightly as I could as the horses ran through the darkness, running wild with no direction or control. I couldn't see where we were or where we were going. All I could do was hang on.

We ran and ran. I could hear the other horses around me in the darkness. Finally, I pulled back on the rope, trying to get Black Horse under control. He slowed and finally trotted and then walked and then stopped. I slipped off his back. My legs were trembling. Around me in the dark, I could hear the other horses snorting and blowing and stopping. "Morven?" one of the men called.

"Here," I said. "Who else is here?"

Other voices began calling through the darkness; one man was missing. That one was Dura.

"Get to our people," I said. "Get everyone up and moving as soon as there is any light. If Dura is still missing, I will go back and look for him. Or perhaps he will find us." There was enough starlight to find our way and soon we saw the fires of our people in the darkness. We came into the camp to general rejoicing.

"Some men will have to watch the horses," I said. "We have no fences here." One of my small sisters took Black Horse's rope. I went to Lani's fire.

"I have to go back," I said. "I heard someone cry out. I think it was Dura."

"Rest and eat first," she said.

"I hit a man with my stick, I saw him fall." I felt sick. I had never hit anyone before.

"Morven, that is not a good thing."

"I was angry," I said.

"But to hit a fellow human, if you hurt him, you hurt his family, you hurt all the people."

"I know," I said. I put down the bowl of stew she handed me. The smell of the food hurt my throat. "No. I have to go back. Oh, Lani, what have I done?"

I stood up and almost ran away. I didn't want Lani to see my face. The crunch of the stick and the face of the man I hit kept reappearing in my head, over and over. I whistled for the spotted dog, who was probably asleep with his kin, and he came soon enough.

"Come with me," I said to him and he followed at my heels. I went back on foot the way we had come. There was a small glimmer of light on the horizon. Dawn would be here soon, but maybe not soon enough. Spotted Dog and I looked for Dura together. I trusted his nose and eyes more than my own.

But I couldn't find Dura. I re-traced my steps as far as the hill outside of Kazaan. As soon as dawn came, they would pick up our trail and come after us. I had to hurry.

I picked up my bundle, and opened it and threw everything out but a sleeping robe, the bow, my bowl and digging stick, and some other tools. Then I hoisted it on my back and stumbled the long distance back again. By the time I got to Lani's fire, I couldn't keep my eyes open; I fell asleep sitting up beside the fire while all around me people were packing and moving. Then after a short nap, I forced myself to my feet, and went to the horses. We packed the children and bundles on the horses and all that day, we walked towards the western sky, through tall grass and past small groves of trees. The hunters stayed behind us, watching for the Kazaans.

When we finally stopped, I went and crawled in with the dogs and went to sleep. I woke abruptly. Lani was sitting and watching me. I knew as soon as I opened my eyes that she was angry and frightened. "Dura is not back. A runner from the Kazaan has been here. He says you killed one of their people."

I sat up abruptly. "No."

"They say you hit him and rode over him on the black horse. They say you are not a human being anymore. They say our elders should make you go away, away from our camp, and away from our people. They say that one who can do what you have done should not live with people."

"Where is Dura?"

"He is in their camp. They say they will send him back when you have gone."

"But, I didn't kill anyone." But then the memory came back, the man's face, the sound of the stick when it hit. "He was in my way. I just wanted to make him move. I didn't kill him," I repeated. But I wasn't sure.

"They say he is dead."

"No. He can't be."

"Morven, I warned you. I said, leave the horses. We could have bargained or traded to get them back. Now I don't know what to do. What if Dura is hurt? What if they don't let him return?" She began to weep.

The sigh of her tears cut me to the heart. This was all my fault. I had let my anger loose in the world and it had returned to hurt Lani.

"I will go away," I said, standing up. "I will live as I lived before. With the dogs. With the horses. They are my relatives too."

"No, Morven, no, you have a human family, you have sisters. You have people who want you to stay here and do the work there is to be done, to keep us all together, so we survive, so we go on being a people, a family, a clan. You can't just leave. We need you. I need you."

"What are you saying to me, Lani? The people of Kazaan say I should leave, that I am not a human being. You want me to stay. Dura needs to come here to be with all of us. You need him to be here as well. What shall I do? What then must I do?"

I put my face in my hands, rocked back and forth. What had I done? What should I do? I was more of an outsider than I had ever been.

"I don't know," she said. She sat down beside me. "I don't know."

"Lani, I was trying to keep us alive, to give us all a gift. I meant only good."

She took my hand. "I don't understand it either. It is as if you have lit a fire in dry grass. Nothing will come right until it has burnt itself out. The Kazaans are different than us. We knew that. But we didn't know how different." She held my hand to her cheek. "Morven, they have different ideas from us, but it is true that in our clan, if one of us hurts another, that person must leave."

"They kept Shuz to work for them." My voice rose. "They say, mine, yours. They make lines on the land with fences. They stay in one place. They brought gifts to my tent all summer, as long as I was teaching them. But when they were done learning, no more gifts. I didn't understand what their gifts meant. I thought they were just gifts." My voice cracked. I turned my head away so Lani wouldn't see my anger, and my fear.

"We must talk to them. We must try to settle this. It will take time, and care," Lani said. "You will have to make amends to the man's family, tell them you intended no harm. But you can't leave us."

"What if it can't be settled?"

"Don't say that. It must be settled." She got to her feet and left. I followed her but she wouldn't look at me. It was late in the day. A red sun was lying on a dusty horizon. Spotted Dog was waiting for me. The dust was from the horses coming into camp with several of the men looking after them.

The people all gathered in a circle around Lani's fire. Everyone had heard. Everyone wanted to speak. We talked, all together, long into the night. Finally a group of people, two men and two women, were chosen to take a selection of the horses back to the Kazaan's. In return, we would ask for Dura, and for a few of their sheep and goats. We worked out the details carefully. It seemed fair. The rest of us waited all day for their return. Finally, near dusk, they came back without the horses. Dura was not with them.

We all gathered around them, waiting for someone to speak. Everyone was silent. "Dura is dead," one of the men said. "They told us he fell from his horse last night. They brought him into a house but he died."

Lani began to wail and some of the other people took it up.

"They are still angry," one of the women cried. "They say bring the all horses back or they will come and get them. That is their only answer. It was that young one, that Kai. He went against the elders and the young men sided with him. The elders say the young men will have their way no matter what they do. The young men no longer listen to them."

People began bickering and yelling at each other. I went away from them, into the darkness, where the horses were tearing grass with their strong teeth, where the baby horses were nursing or playing and the mothers turned to lick them. I stood beside the black horse, who was only eating occasionally. The rest of the time he stood with his nose to the wind, his nostrils flaring, testing the wind, his dark eyes staring into darkness. He paid little attention to me.

After a while, I went further into the darkness. I had no idea what to do or where to go. I found myself under the trees; I could hear water running. I went forward until I could see the glint of water in the starlight. The full moon was coming. I sat on the grass and listened to the wind in the trees. It seemed to me to contain the voice of my mother. I had seen her dead body but perhaps whatever had made my mother move and breathe and talk and sing was still close. The elders taught us that death was only a change; that the dead were still around us but in a different world.

"Mother," I said. "What shall I do?"

But I heard only leaves in the wind. Now the anger and fear were draining out of me like water from a waterskin, and I felt flabby and empty. In some way I didn't understand, I had made a terrible mistake. I wasn't even sure what the mistake was and I couldn't see any way to put it right.

I fell asleep with my back against a tree. When I woke, the sun was in my eyes, my mouth was dry, and my hair had come loose from its braid. I felt like a fool, sitting there with a string of spit on my chin, dusty and dirty and ashamed. But I still didn't know what to do.

Suddenly I heard a yell, then a series of screams and yells. I knew instantly what had happened. The Kazaans had come, as they promised, to fight for the horses. I heard hooves on the grass. I ran as fast as I could, burst out of the trees and up the hill to where the horses were milling back and forth. A Kazaan had a rope over the black horse's neck; the black horse was fighting and pulling to get away. Other Kazaans were grabbing at the rest of the horses. The two men who had been guarding the horses were swinging sticks in a futile attempt to stop the Kazaans. Other men were running from our camp but they would not be in time.

I ran as hard as I could. The man holding Black Horse didn't see me coming. I hit him with my own stick with all my strength and he fell. At the same time, I grabbed Black Horse's mane, swung onto his back, and dug my feet hard into his side. He jumped forward and I swung him in circle and then we charged into the middle of the men struggling to catch and hold the horses. The men fell away from in front of us as we charged through and I leant over from Black Horse's back and grabbed a longer heavier stick from one of them. I dragged it from his surprised hand. I whirled the stick over my head and I turned Black Horse and we charged them again. This time, I didn't hesitate. I swung hard with my stick and felt it connect. One of the men I had hit fell down and the other stumbled away, holding his side.

Now all the horses were wild and charging with us; they wanted only to stay with the black horse, their leader. They broke away from the men who were trying to catch them and followed us, wild and kicking and furious, over the hills and away, far away, away. It was all I could think of to do.

Chapter Nine

I sat on the ground with my arms wrapped around my knees. My whole body hurt but it wasn't just physical pain. What hurt was that I had betrayed my people, and that I couldn't face them again. I had done what I told Luz I would do. I had done my best for the people and I had walked my own path. I had failed at both.

Dura was dead. Lani would be right to blame me for that. And I had killed someone without meaning to. Perhaps more people had been hurt in the last fight over the horses. I didn't know. I remembered one of the men staggering away after I had hit him. And it had been so much easier to swing a stick the second time around.

The Kazaans were right. When someone killed someone else in our clan, they were forced to leave. We couldn't afford that kind of madness among the people.

Once I thought I wanted to be alone, but being alone when I had the choice of going back to my mother's warm tent, or to my own tent with people all around me, was very different than being alone on the flat and endless plains, with winter coming on and no sense of how I would survive it. I had left everything behind, not just the people, including Lani, Shuz, and the Kazaan's with their snarling faces, but everything. All the tools I needed to survive—

my bow, my tent, my sleeping robes, my water skins—were back in a bundle in the camp. I should take the horses back, go back, gather my things and say farewell.

But I wasn't going back there. I felt sick even thinking about it. I had betrayed my people. I had killed someone.

Plus, I had no real idea where Lani and the people were. The horses and I had run until they were exhausted. Then we had all stopped. I fell off Black Horse and lay curled on the ground. Every time I closed my eyes, I saw the violence in front of me, the men's faces, the rearing horses. I heard Lani, from a distance, screaming something I couldn't hear. Over and over, I felt the stick in my hand, felt it connect to someone, felt the sting of it in my arm. I felt sick. I doubled over and threw up. I sat with my head on my knees, rocking and rocking. Then I got up, got back on Black Horse, and we moved on again.

I kept them moving, even though all the horses wanted was to go back to a land and a territory that was familiar, where they knew how to survive. I made them keep going; west, west, we went, every day, drifting and eating. I didn't eat.

When it was finally clear in my head that I wasn't going back, I began looking for a place we could stay for the winter. The horses, as least, needed water and shelter, trees, tall grass, a river or stream. They needed a place where they could survive by digging through the snow to get to the grass and by stripping the bark off trees. If there was fish, or small animals, I could survive as well. Or not. I wasn't sure I cared about surviving anymore.

After many days of journeying slowly over the flat plains, we came to an edge. A steep walled canyon yawned beneath me. Far below, I could see the glint of water. There was a river down there. We found an animal trail and went over the edge, down and down through the weathered stones and twisted gravel columns and bent trees, down until we came out onto a level area full of brush and open space beside the river. It was what we needed. It would do.

I left the horses to their own explorations and made a camp for myself by a bend in the river where the water curled into itself and made a dark pool. I washed and then hunted up and down the river's edge until I found the right kind of flint. I spent some time bent over the flint chipping it until I had an edge that would cut. Then I carefully cut a piece off the bottom of my leather shirt for a string. I found a springy piece of wood and tied on the string to make a bow drill to finally have a fire. I hadn't had to do this for a long while. I had forgotten how boring and time consuming it was. Finally, a tiny curl of smoke rose up from the wood dust on the piece of bark between my feet. When I had a fire, I relaxed a little. Now the trick was not to let it go out again. When my people travelled, we always carried fire with us, tucked inside smoldering moss within in a clay container.

I broke off pieces of wood from the jumble of driftwood logs beside the river, piled it beside the fire, sat staring into the fire while darkness fell over the land. I sat while the evening wind bent the trees and rustled the water, while small animals skittered through the brush and night birds swooped overhead. Eventually I fell asleep that way, with my head on my chest. I woke, added wood to the fire and curled on the sandy cold ground, but this time I didn't sleep. Instead, images from the fight with the Kazaans exploded in my head, as they had done for days, until eventually I got up and rummaged in the darkness for more wood, anything to keep the pictures away. But of course it didn't work.

Finally, I sat and stared into the flames and tried to think, as I had before, of how things had gone so wrong, of why my good intentions had broken my family into pieces, of what the elders of the Kazaans had meant, what I could have said to them but didn't, of what they had said to me—words that repeated themselves over and over and over until I held my head in my hands, tempted to bang it with a rock if only it would just please be quiet.

Eventually I fell asleep again, and woke curled on the sandy ground as dawn crept over the valley. At first I was surprised to feel a warm body next to mine and then I felt his bony background and ribs and realized that the spotted dog, faithful and tireless, had found me, even though I had run away from him without a word. He must have been following us the whole time. I scratched his ears and he licked my face and then shook himself and went off to hunt. I knew I should do the same. I had eaten almost nothing during the days when we had been travelling, a few shrivelled berries, some roots, eaten raw rather than cooked, but no meat. I hadn't wanted to take the time to hunt. The horses had lost weight as well. They would be off tearing at the grass, eating as much as they could, trying to put on a layer of fat before the cold came.

The dog came back with a small fat brown rodent and dumped it at my feet. I skinned and cooked it and gave him half.

Then we set off to explore. I followed the river downstream. After several hours of fighting my way through thick brush, I came a place where the canyon opened up and the river widened into a lake. At the river's entry into the lake were wide reed beds. Ducks squawked and preened themselves among the reeds. Fish rising dimpled the lake's surface. The lake was set in a round bowl of humped green hills, rising in a series of flat ledges up to the plains. I would need roots for snares, sticks for spears to catch fish. Maybe I could hollow out a log for a canoe.

But first, and most importantly, I needed a den. Without a tent, I had to have some kind of shelter. We went back upriver and the next day, I spent the whole day looking until I found a sheltered corner of the canyon wall, beneath a thick grove of trees. The sandy ground was easy to dig, the river wasn't far away. I would have some shelter from the wind and snow and an easy source of wood.

Over the next few weeks, I tried to create the tools and materials that I needed to survive the winter. I knew I didn't have much time. I dug a hole with my hands, into the gravel bank and covered it with logs and leaves. I dragged in as much wood as I could find, knowing it wouldn't be nearly enough to last and I would probably be searching for wood under the snow. I built snares from green branches and caught rabbits and other small animals, and once, very luckily, a half-grown deer so that I had a hide to work with. I went back up to the plains and frantically dug for tubers but it was too late. The tops had all dried, and they were too hard to find. I speared fish and dried them. I found some clay and made water jugs and bowls but the clay was sandy, and they broke too easily. I did what I could. It was very little.

I made a bed of logs and covered it with leaves and heaps of dried grass and then laid the deer hide over it. I needed moccasins, I needed warm clothes; I needed so many things. Mostly I needed my family. But I wouldn't think about that. I couldn't think about that. If I did, I might lie down on the grass and never get up again. Mostly I worked myself to exhaustion so I could sleep without visions, without images, without nightmares.

The days continued warm. I had almost relaxed and then one night, in my sleep, I felt the wind change. I could feel the cold crawling under my hide clothes, crawling over the land, freezing everything in its path. I spent that day huddled over the fire, unable to get warm. The cold seemed to cut through me. That night, when I tried to sleep, the cold bit at my feet and hands. I sat up and put more wood on the fire. I dozed, sitting, by the fire, and in the morning, I forced myself to stand, to run, and when the cold got too much, I went back to the fire.

The river froze far more quickly than I expected. The horses worked at keeping a waterhole open and so did I. I got into the habit of going to the river several times a day, smashing the thin new ice with a pole. But the river froze faster than I could keep it open. It froze up from the bottom of the river, froze up to the hole so that the water flowed over the ice and made it almost impossible to walk on.

And then it snowed. And snowed. It snowed for days. At least it was warmer when it snowed and it made my small shelter windproof, but it made wood for the fire, and grass for the horses, harder and harder to find. The horses grew thin. I grew thin. The spotted dog did better than the rest of us, since there were still small animals beneath the snow that he could find. He and I shared the dried fish, I heated water for tea, and we curled together in the miserable nights to sleep.

Finally the snow relented, the sun came out, and water ran and trickled and dripped on everything, ran through the leaves on the shelter and soaked my bed. The fire smoked and spat at me, refusing to burn. At least it was warm enough that my hands and feet no longer froze and burned and split.

And then the cold came back and froze the world into ice.

Now the horses were really in trouble. Snow they could paw through, but the ice cut their legs and feet. And the cold took their strength. Mostly they stood still, their heads down, keeping the spark of life alive deep inside themselves.

I began to cut long branches of willow and haul them to the horses. It wasn't much but it was something. It took all my strength to cut through the trees with my dull knife, to break and twist them and drag them through the snow to the horses. My legs were cut and bleeding as well. The horses could eat snow for water and I could thaw snow and ice in a clay bowl by the fire, but still I was always thirsty.

I could feel myself getting weaker every day. The day came when all the roots and all the dried berries and fish were gone. I stripped bark from the willow trees and boiled it but it was a bitter tea and I gagged on it. I was dying. I could feel it. All the strength in my body was going into just keeping a bit of warmth in my belly and now even that was fading. I didn't really care anymore. It was all such a struggle and for what? That's what I couldn't understand: why I was trying so hard. I wanted to give up and something wouldn't let me.

And then, one evening, I lay on the bed, cold to my heart's core, under the rotten deer hide, and I began to drift. And then I began to dream. I could no longer tell what was real and what wasn't, and I didn't much care.

I began to feel warm. I could smell the familiar smells of home, the smoky reek of the cured hides on the tents, the smell of dried grass underneath my bed. And then my mother came and sat down with me. She touched my hand. I heard her voice. I could smell her familiar smell, a smell I loved and had missed so much, more even, than I had realized. I couldn't see her because for some reason, I couldn't open my eyes.

"You did well, my daughter," she said. I wept then, for I didn't understand why she was saying this. I hadn't done well and I still didn't understand; I still didn't know why it had all gone so wrong. She took my hand and I rose from the freezing damp bed and went with her. We rose gently into the air. We flew over the frozen white land but I was warm. My mother's hand in mine sent strength and warmth all through me.

"Look, Morven. The world shifts and flows like water in a stream," my mother said. And indeed the world beneath us shifted and changed as we flew, from winter to summer and back again. I didn't understand how I could see all this with my eyes closed, but somehow I could.

"Sometimes it flows easily; sometimes it curls in on itself. Sometime it is blocked and it changes course and flows another way. You changed the water's flow, my daughter. You brought a new thing into the world, and no one knew how to think about this thing. Some people thought one way about it, some people another, according to their natures. You did no wrong. It is hard for people to change."

We flew over the village of the Kazaans. Smoke curled from the roofs. People were going about their lives. The sheep and goats were in their pens but there was another pen, full of horses. So Dura had died for nothing. All the fighting had been about nothing. They had simply replaced the horses I took with others. The ones we had given them stood peacefully in pens. Their village looked peaceful, and I realized it wasn't the horses they had wanted. I had taken something more valuable: their pride in themselves, their sense of their way of life as better than ours. No wonder they had hated me.

I looked at the Kazaans walking around. There was the man I had supposedly killed, going toward the horse pen. He looked up and I saw his face clearly. "Mother—" I began, but she pulled me onwards.

We flew farther and higher, towards the sun, and then my mother became a bright light, brighter even than the sun, until her hand grew too hot and began to burn me and I let go. I awoke, fevered and cold, and weeping, on the bed. I didn't want to be there. I wanted to be flying with my mother, free and warm and alive. I curled my knees tightly into my chest to stop shaking. But a part of me was joyous, full of light. My mother had come. She wasn't gone. She wasn't angry at me. She hadn't left me. I held this thought close to me, and it warmed me.

Eventually I fell asleep again—or passed out—and dreamed again. I dreamed that Lani and I were young; we knew each other and played together. We were sitting by a stream and sun beat down through the leaves onto our heads and faces. We were making rope together out of dried grass, we spun it and wove it and spun and made a great golden rope that shone like the sun. We played a game where we wrapped the rope around our wrists and arms and hands, and finally, Lani untangled it and threw it up into the sky.

"Catch it, Morven," she called to me. I was laughing. I jumped up to catch the rope but it stayed just out of my reach. "Don't worry, it will wait there for you," she said. She was laughing too. Her face was light and joyous. "It will be there when you need it, all you have to do is catch it and hold on."

I reached again for the rope but it was too high, just out of reach, and I couldn't run after it any longer. I had no strength. Then I woke up again.

This time, something warm was licking my face. I reached out, felt the bony hide, It was the spotted dog, thin but warm. Carefully, he lay down, curled up at my side; I curled around his warm body and put my arms around him. It helped. I stopped shaking. I dreamed again.

This time I dreamed of Dura. We were in the desert again, and there was the huge tiger but this time it was friendly. It purred and played with us. It was shining as well. It was astonishingly huge and then it lay down, and Dura and I climbed on its back. I held on to Dura as the tiger sprang into the sky.

"You see," he said to me, turning and smiling. "I am feeling well now. I am so much stronger. I am going on a journey and you will not see me again, but remember me. Think of me. Tell the children."

And then he was gone, and I was falling and falling. It seemed to me I fell for days and days and when I finished falling, I was lying beside the spotted dog, and a thin finger of sunlight was reaching in towards me. I tried to sit up and couldn't. I was so tired. I couldn't seem to wake up. I lay there wondering why I was still alive, and why I wasn't flying with my mother or Dura. I missed them and I didn't want to be here in this cold, mould-mud-stinking, wet-dog world. I turned my head, and there, carefully laid beside my head, was a dead rabbit.

I stared at it and it stared back with its dead yellow eyes.

I thought about how much effort it would be to sit up and cook the rabbit and eat it. I thought about the golden rope binding Lani and me. I thought about my mother turning into the sun and Dura's smile. I thought about the Kazaan man, walking around, still alive.

I sat up.

Outside the shelter, sun was pouring down. The snow was softening, and water was dripping off the gravel bank above me. I dug carefully through the ashes of my fire until, deep down, I found a spark. I took some of the grass and dried leaves from my bed and laid them on the spark until a tiny golden flame spurted up. Carefully, and with enormous effort, I pulled out some of the sticks that had made up my bed and laid their ends in the fire, so they made a flame. They were dry and burned easily.

The bowl beside the fire was full of water. I drank and drank and then set it in the warm ashes. It took me a while to get to my feet and I had to hold onto the edge of the shelter.

I am alive, I thought. *For today, at least, I am alive.*

I took one careful step and then another and stood in a shaft of bright sunlight. It held some warmth. I staggered towards the river and then at its edge, I stopped. The ice had loosened its grip.

The river was very low and in the pools that were free of ice, I could see schools of fish, many trapped by the shallow water.

The spotted dog galloped down the bank, ran into the water, grabbed a fish, dragged it up on the bank, tore it open and gulped the fat along the spine. He ate a bit more flesh, and then dived for another fish and again, ate the fatty parts. I picked up the fish he had left and sat on the ground. Slowly and carefully, I ate small bits of the raw flesh. I stopped often to rest and then I ate some more. There was fat under the skin and I licked that down.

I sat there on the sandy bank, in the sun, all day, watching the river run, eating bits of fish. I dozed and then ate. When night came, I gathered pieces of wood and took them back to the fire. I picked bits and pieces of plants and bark and put them in the water and heated it and drank a bowl of tea and then another one.

The next day I made a fish spear. I ate more fish and then I began to gather fish and dry them.

Every day I got stronger. I found the horses, who had all survived. They had spent part of the winter trapped under the trees by the deep snow. They were thin but mats of dried hair were falling off them and they were eating everything they could find to eat, willow branches, tree bark, and brush. I said hello to them all and then went back to the fish.

The next day it rained and the day after that. I sat in my shelter, watching it rain, while cakes of ice floated down the river. I had gathered dry wood and I made tea and ate more fish and dreamed some more.

On the morning of the fourth day of rain, I woke early because the sound of the river had changed. I sprang up and ran down to the river. Instead of being clear and rushing, it was now grey and twisted, curling back on itself, almost to the top of the banks and obviously still rising. Something had happened to the river. There was no time to wonder what. Because the river was rising so fast, I knew had to get the horses out of the valley.

I ran back to the den, grabbed the string of dried fish, my knife, the deer hide, and threw some coals from the fire into a clay bowl. I ran through the brush with my awkward burden. The horses were where I had last seen them.

It took me many frustrating minutes to coax the black horse to let me on his back and then to get them to follow us. The horses were nervous and panicky; they knew something was wrong and so they ran in circles in the wrong direction and it took us all a while to find the trail up the bank where we had come down so long ago. It was a hard struggle to get up; the bank was muddy and slippery and each animal coming up made the trail worse.

After we were up, I sat on the high bank and watched the river eat up the place where we had been. I didn't care. The sun was warm on my back; there were tiny blades of new green grass springing from the ground. The horses spread out and ate like starving things. Even the spotted dog chewed on the grass. I lay on the grass and then I took my ragged bits of clothes off and rolled and rolled like a horse. Bits of dried skin fell off my back and hands and shoulders; I had grown a second skin and now I was shedding it in the sun. I ate a bit of fish and then I found a dry and sandy spot and curled up and went to sleep.

Chapter Ten

So I hadn't died, and I no longer wanted to be alone. What should I do? Most of all, I needed to find out if my dream had been true, if the Kazaan man was still alive.

The next morning, I sat and faced the new sun. I made a tiny fire and put bits of green plants on the flame so the smoke curled and wavered and made loops around my head. Luz had told me once that the smoke from certain plants would carry my spirit into the other world. I closed my eyes and faced east, into the sun, and thought about Lani. I visualized everything I could remember, her black hair, her serious brown eyes, the sound of her voice, her ragged leather clothes, the new baby, her voice, scolding, advising, counselling. I thought of the golden rope hanging just over my head and I tried to see myself jumping up and catching it but I couldn't quite make it.

The more I thought about Lani, my mother, the other people of the clan, the lonelier I got. I missed my little sisters. I missed Shuz. I had no idea what had happened to her—or to anyone else, for that matter.

The spotted dog growled and I opened my eyes. I had been concentrating so hard on Lani and my people that, at first, I wasn't surprised to see a distant line of figures crossing the horizon. Then I woke up. After my experience at Kazaan, I no longer trusted people in the same way. I had never been so hurt by other people before, never been attacked. I had never even considered the possibility. And yet now I longed more than anything else to fling myself, running, over the flat ground to these people, to walk with them and talk with them and sit down around the fire and eat, laugh, sing, play drums. This surprised me because all my life, I thought that I wanted to avoid people and be alone. And now I was feeling a whole new feeling that I couldn't describe; it was like being a drop of water without a river to belong to. Dry somehow, and desperate. But I didn't make a sound. I didn't wave. I waited and watched, silent, with a hand on the spotted dog's side to keep him from barking until they were out of sight. I hoped they wouldn't see or smell my tiny fire.

I was curious and I considered following them. But it had been a line of upright figures, no one carrying bundles, no bent figures with loads on their backs, no children. So it was probably hunters, men with weapons, and I had had enough of them. And something about their movements and their silhouettes told me they were not of my clan.

But I couldn't stand my own solitude any longer either. I thought about what to do. I could try to retrace my steps, to try and track where my family had gone. Had Shuz gone with them? She wasn't happy at Kazaan. Or perhaps she had gone looking for her own family.

Or had the fighting continued? Perhaps my people had been hurt, even killed. Would the Kazaan do that? I thought of Lani and then I thought of Lani's baby, who I had promised to protect. I had run away when my people needed me. First I had let my anger goad me into a foolish strategy, and then instead of facing what had happened, I had run away.

And yet, my mother was with me. She had told me I had done well.

I stood up, I turned around and around in a wide circle. The hunters had disappeared and I was alone again. There was a kind of enormous emptiness about this land. The huge sky. The sun hanging above me. The wind blowing out of the south. Very faintly I could hear the rumble and roar of the river below me. I had the sun and the river and the wind and the sky.

But where in all this land was Lani? More than anything, I wanted to tell her about my winter, about the dreams, about flying with Dura. I had to tell her that Dura's spirit was well, that he was getting better and that he had gone on to a new land. She would be so happy to know that.

But how to find her? And for the first time in my life, I felt really lost. I had no idea which way to go, where my family might be. I might never find them again. I might travel and travel all over this enormous land, I might go around in circles and up and down and in and out for all my future days and not find what I sought.

And now, finally, I knew fear. All my life, people had talked about fear and I had never cared. My mother had tried to tell me to be careful; my mother was always fearful and careful, but never foolishly. She had taught me, or tried to teach me. She had told me stories of how the world was made to which I had never really listened. Now I looked at what I knew, at the fact that I knew nothing except that I was alive in a flat and endless world, and afraid.

When I was dying in my cave-den, I hadn't cared and I didn't mind if I died. But now I had something to live for. I wanted to find out if the Kazaan man was really alive. I wanted to find Lani and my people and apologize and ask them to take me back. They might refuse. They would be right to refuse. I was afraid of their faces, of their anger, of their refusal. But I had to ask.

But I am not a person who can sit down and spend time just being afraid. I couldn't stand it. I had to do something even if that something achieved nothing. I went to find the horses. The black horse saw me coming, came and bowed his head in greeting and then went back to eating. They were all eating and eating and rolling to get off the dead hair and winter mud and then going back to eating like the half-starved creatures they were.

Black Horse needed to stay with his mares and their babies. He needed to look after his family. I picked out two new horses to travel with. Over the next few days, I got them used to me, to the rope and to being touched and ridden. It didn't take long to get these two young male horses, one gold and one grey, used to being ridden. And then, finally, one morning, I said goodbye to Black Horse, who didn't know it was good bye, who rubbed his beautiful sleek black head against mine and then went back to eating.

I turned my back on him and his family. The two young horses didn't want to leave but I persuaded them. They were old enough that the black horse would soon have driven them away. I headed east and north. If the people had gone away from Kazaan, they might even have followed my trail. They would have had to find somewhere to overwinter. There would be signs; what I would have to do is look, watch the spotted dog, who knew so much more than me, and who would find the trail, the scent, or the sounds. Compared to him, I was blind and deaf.

Over the next few days, as we worked our way slowly over the land, I stopped often to eat; I seemed to be always hungry and there was plenty of food: bird's eggs, fish in the creeks, bulbs and tubers, fresh green shoots of reeds. I stopped to make a bow; that took me several days and even then it wasn't made properly. I didn't have the right leather for the strings or the right stones for the arrowheads, but it would do for now. I needed something more as covering for my body as well and I stopped long enough to hunt a deer, stretch and scrape the hide, and cut into something serviceable. I made better ropes for the horses; one day I found a streambed with the right kind of flintstone and I spent several days making a proper knife. It was slow and exacting work, but I was happy with it when I was done. Then I made a holder for the knife as well.

With the hide of the next deer, I made a kind of pad to fit on the back of the horses, tied on with rope. I still had no tent, no cooking pots or baskets, no sleeping robes. I slept on the ground by the fire, with the spotted dog keeping my back warm. On nights that it rained, I sheltered where I could, under trees, or where there were no trees, under a sloping bank or behind a rock. I was often cold and wet but I learned to carefully watch the wind and clouds, to watch for places of shelter, to always be prepared. The weather in this place was sudden and violent and always changing; the wind swept the clouds past and away. Sometimes I would be sitting in the sun watching a distant storm sweep by; sometimes I would be riding in the rain towards bright sunlight. Shadows and colours swept over the grass; birds circled overhead. Herds of deer and other horned animals wandered in front of us.

But always I was watching the ground, watching the horizon, watching the spotted dog, searching for signs, sounds, smells. And then one day I cut across a trail where people had passed not too many days earlier. I stopped, studied the tracks, then turned in the same direction they had been travelling. Their tracks puzzled me; some things were familiar and some were not. They had animals with them, sheep and goats, but not horses. They probably weren't Kazaan people because they never left their solid houses. But it wasn't my family, I was pretty sure of that.

There were women and children, and they were obviously carrying some fairly large loads, I could see that from the places where they had stopped to rest.

By the evening of the second day, I found the place where recently, perhaps a few days ago, these strange people had stopped to camp. And then on the third day, I crossed yet another group of tracks, from the south, that fell into the trail of the first. And then a third group came in from the north. What was going on?

I followed, slowly, not wanting to be seen. And then when several more groups of tracks joined up, I finally got it.

It was a Gathering. It had to be.

In the country we had left, we had a Gathering every two or three years. Someone would decide the time and place, some elder or wise seer, and runners would be sent out, young men and women, to find the scattered tribes and call them together. It would take many, many days, sometimes half a year, to find everyone and call them together and several more spans of time for everyone to agree to come.

There were many reasons for calling such a Gathering, and many reasons for all of us to go. They lasted for many days and in that time, women became pregnant, ideas, stories, songs, goods, and anything else we had or needed was exchanged or learned or taught. There were fights and laughter and foolishness and then we went away again, changed and renewed, to our separate, wandering lives.

I followed the broad flowing trails of tracks as they gathered and intersected, and then one day I saw on the horizon the many thin trails of smoke and dust that told me a huge group of people were near. Spotted Dog growled and growled, deep in his throat and the two young horses curved their necks in fear. I stopped and camped. I wasn't quite ready to be among a lot of strange people I knew nothing about.

I tied the horses and walked to the top of a hill. The camp was in a large extended bowl of land with a river and low hills all around. I could look out over the ranks of tents and fires and people moving around or sitting in circles or walking or talking or eating. I watched for a long time, shivering just a little, both afraid and excited.

And then I saw them, so distant, they were just tiny figures, but still, I was fairly sure: Lani and Shuz, and the children, and the rest of the people of my clan. I sat on the hill with my head in my hands. They had made it through the winter, and somehow they had met and made friends with other new people who were not the Kazaans.

What would they think? Would they blame me? Were they angry? Would Lani look at me in sorrow and fear? Could I live with her anger, her blaming me for Dura's death?

And so far, there was no sign of the Kazaans. Maybe they weren't coming. Had Dura's people come? Usually, in a Gathering, all the clans were included. But perhaps the Kazaans didn't want to be with other people. Perhaps they couldn't leave their houses and their animals.

I looked back at the empty plain behind me. I couldn't go back into that great blue shadowed loneliness and mystery by myself ever again. Despite how difficult I found it to be with people, being alone was worse. Plus, just surviving by myself was hard. I'm like a horse, I thought, I have to be with my kind, even when it hurts.

And then there were the horses. Did I want to go through all that again? Bringing horses to these new people, showing them what to do and how to be friends with horses and how to ride and then seeing people fight over them?

What had my mother said, that I had changed the shape of the river and it would never be the same? But still, the river, even when it changed its shape, was still the same river.

I sighed, and again put my face in my hands. I wanted this choice to pass me by. I wanted to lie here in the sun on this hilltop forever and perhaps turn over on my back and watch the birds circling and wheeling overhead, watch the clouds form and move as the wind took them. Perhaps I could lie here on the edge of things, neither in the world nor out of it, neither dead nor alive, not in pain, not anything, just a speck of dust lying on the grass like all the other specks of dust.

And I did lie there for a long time. I was so tired. I watched the birds and the clouds and the sun, wondering about them all, and then eventually I had to pee and I was hungry and thirsty and my skin was burning. I thought of sleeping all night in a tent with a full belly, wrapped in warm fur, next to a fire that never needed wood because someone else would go get it and tend the fire and cook the food and do the hunting.

I thought of talking to Lani about my mother and about the golden rope and how Dura was well.

I rolled over and got to my feet. I went and got the two horses and I rode down the hill and over the plain and across the long rolling flat and then up another small hill and then through the ring of tents to Lani's tent, where I slid off in front of her. She had seen me coming and was standing, waiting. Shuz stood in the door of the tent.

People came running. Everyone had seen me coming. They were all babbling to each other. They gathered in a circle around us and stared and muttered among themselves and finally fell silent.

"Well," she said finally. "You're back. You're alive. You survived."

"Yes," I said. I stood in front of her with my head down, not looking at her, just waiting. "Lani, I am so sorry," I began.

"Morven," she interrupted me, and sighed.

"Yes?"

"Oh, come and sit down, come inside, come and lie down, come and eat, you fool, you stupid, silly, foolish, stupid, skinny..."

Now I looked and she was both laughing and crying at the same time.

"You look like a starved dog," she said.

I took a step forward but it was hard to walk...I started to fall and then she leaned forward and caught me and then many hands caught me as well and I felt myself being carried inside the tent. I curled up into the softness of furs. I was warm, warm at last.

Someone spooned soup down my throat and I gagged and swallowed and then I slept.

In the night I woke and my mother sat beside me smiling, tossing a loop of golden rope, a glowing circle in her hands and then she faded away and I went back to sleep. I began to grow too hot and I kicked the furs away and then I was freezing and I pulled them back but now I couldn't get warm. I began to shake and someone spooned warm meat broth down my throat and I slept again, but now my dreams had changed. There were no golden ropes, just strange billowing shapes and animals with teeth and giant snakes that grew and then faded. I tossed and turned. I wanted to wake up, but I couldn't move. I thought perhaps I had been captured by the Kazaans, and I began to fight and struggle and hit at whatever was holding me, but I had no strength. Whoever I was hitting only laughed and nothing I could do seemed to hurt them. I was so cold. Perhaps I was back in the cave. Perhaps I really had died and all the travelling and warmth and sun had only been another dream.

That thought scared me so much I woke up. I was in the tent, the beautiful tent, with a fire burning and from far away, I could hear voices and people and children laughing. I was desperately thirsty and I needed to pee but when I tried to stand up, for some reason my legs didn't work very well and then I got tangled up in the fur robes some-

how and fell over again. It took me a while to get untangled, and then I crawled over to the poles on the side of the tent and pulled myself up and staggered to the doorway and fell through it onto the ground.

People I didn't know came and then Lani was at my side. Sweat was running down my face but the sun was bright and I only wanted to stand there and let it take the deep, deep chill from my bones. Then I remembered.

"Have to pee," I muttered. Lani and someone else helped me to the back of the tent where I peed in the grass and then they helped me back to the bed and brought me water and I went to sleep again.

When I woke again, I lay still for a while. My body felt weak but it worked. When I moved my legs out from under the fur, I was dizzy but at least I could sit. Standing took a bit longer but I managed. This time I made it out the door on my own and sat down by the fire.

Lani came quickly. She brought me a bowl of food. I was starving. I ate one bowl and asked for another. Lani's food always tasted better than other people's; she flavoured it with leaves and bits of salt.

"Wait a bit," she said. "You've been asleep and sick for many, many days."

"The horses…"

"The children have taken good care of them."

"What is this?" I waved my arm at the circle of tents.

She frowned. "It's a Gathering. We were fortunate. We met people on the plains. We found new friends and they invited us. This Gathering is almost done. We have been here long enough. We are talking about the Kazaans. They were not invited here."

I waited.

"There is something strange about them," Lani said. "Of course, our people found that out, but now I have found that other people of these plains also find them difficult. Many people avoid them. A few trade with them."

I looked a question.

"It is so hard to understand. The elders and shamans have been going through the old stories and songs. They say the Kazaans are like two-headed people, like people who have clouds in their eyes and can't see or hear properly. They hear things other people don't hear, they say things that don't make sense."

"What are they saying?"

"The Kazaans have a strong language but their words are different from ours. Remember how they talked about owning. Now they have taken some people away from their families and made them do the work for the Kazaan. They say that having the horses makes them different. The horses make them stronger and faster. That, at least, is true."

"But we have horses too."

"Yes," she said. "Now that you are here, you can help us get some more horses. We have no choice. We need to get enough horses so we can travel far away from these Kazaans. The other people here are like us. They trade, they are sharing, they are friendly. So now we must decide. Should we travel further? Should we leave this land as well and go farther away?"

"Why should we leave? This is a good land. In the valley where I spent the winter is a river full of fish. There is a lake. There is food and shelter and many places where we can live. Remember the dry land, the desert? We can't go back there. We will stay here. There is room enough for everyone."

"The Kazaans have hurt people who try to stop them. They have become cruel in their craziness."

I was silent. It was still hard to understand.

"But what is owning?" I said finally. "It is so strange. When Shuz was there, she did work for them but they gave her food and a place to sleep. How was she owned?"

"They are angry she left. They have sent messages to say she must come back."

"But if she doesn't want to, how can they make her?"

"By hurting her. By hurting us."

I frowned, thinking hard. "The dogs fight sometimes, over food or mating, or who is boss. But as soon as one stops fighting, the other stops. The fight is over. The horses too. Black Horse fought with the young males until they ran away. Then he stopped. There is no owning or hurting. But," I continued, "if a dog doesn't stop fighting then it gets hurt, sometimes it gets killed. If the young males didn't run away, Black Horse would kill them. I have seen this. So perhaps the Kazaans are like this, they have forgotten how to stop fighting. Perhaps we have to hurt them, to remind them."

"Morven, what happens when the horses keep fighting and Black Horse loses?"

"Then he would have to run away or die."

"Exactly. We must run away from these horrible Kazaans, far, far away, or we will have to fight them. And if we fight them and lose, then we will die."

"And if we fight and win, then they will have to run away and leave us alone in peace."

"Morven, it is not worth it. We are not people who fight. To hurt other people, could you do that?"

I thought back to that night at the Kazaan settlement, to the man I had run over with Black Horse.

"Yes," I said, "I did. I could again if I had to. But only if they made me. Only if they were going to hurt you or the children or Shuz." I paused. "What do the men say?"

"Some want to fight. They are angry. That is what we have all been trying to decide. But no one can decide. Some say fight.

Some say leave. We have been here talking for so many hands of days. No one can agree." She paused. "Could we risk it? Getting hurt. Children being hurt? I say no. I have said no. If I have to, I will take the children and leave."

"By yourself?"

"Yes."

"Lani, don't do that...you don't know what it's like. Being alone. Being on your own."

"But Morven, you like to be alone. You have always said so."

"Alone on the edge of camp is one thing. Alone with no one anywhere is another."

"Ah," Lani said softly. "Yes, there is that."

She took my hand in hers. "Morven, I was angry with you for a long time and now I am sorry. I can see now that what happened was no one's fault. You did your best, and so did I, and so did Dura. I am not angry. You are my true sister, the sister of my heart. I am so glad you found your way back to us."

We sat together in silence for a long time. Eventually the children found us and then there were hugs and hair pulling and noise and eating, and no more discussion. The children brought the two horses and tied them close. Other people began to drift towards our fire. They brought food and drums and soon there was singing and dancing. Many people looked at me, but no one asked me anything. I knew there was whispering going on about who I was and from where I might have come.

People joked and laughed. Many people were getting ready to leave the next day. I got very sleepy and I thought of the fur robes in the tent. I stood up and I was walking towards the tent when I saw him, silhouetted against the edge of the sky.

There was only one man, on horseback, and then, suddenly there were more and more. The dogs had seen them now and set up a furious clamour. People were scrambling to their feet, yelling at each other, some were running, some were standing, open-mouthed.

The men on the horses began to move, faster and then faster, their spears held level. I dived for the tent, where the children were sleeping; I had no weapon, I only had a bone knife, I needed a spear. And then I remembered; I had seen a spear earlier that afternoon, in my dazed sleep, casually stashed in the poles of the tent. I found it, I grabbed it, I ran outside to the tethered horses, yanked furiously at the ropes, got them loose, slid on a slick back, yanked the horse's head around, headed straight towards the charging men. I opened my mouth and a noise I didn't recognize came out of my throat, a roar and a scream like that of a charging tiger. I aimed my horse at the largest rider, the one in the middle.

Things seemed to slow and flow around me. The world went quiet. There was me on my crazed and terrified horse, there was the man in front of me, his mouth open, his long back hair in braids flying behind him, his arm raised, holding a spear. I knew his face. I knew him. It was Kai.

And I knew I had to fight him. I no longer had a choice. My place was with my people and I had to defend them.

The white bone blade of his spear shone in the moonlight. It was longer than my spear, which was short and light, suitable for fish or rabbits. He swung it at me and I ducked, flew past him and as I flew, I slid my spear smoothly under his leg, lifted and flipped him off his horse. He fell and rolled but I paid little attention. I was already yanking my horse's head around, turning, spotting my next target. By now, the leading edge of the horsemen had reached the tents. There weren't that many of them; they must have counted on surprising us. They slashed at the tents, at anyone they saw running. I saw one man go down under a horse; I saw a woman knocked over, and then I was behind the men and then I took my silly fishing spear and stuck it in a man's back and my horse jumped over him as he fell.

My stomach churned. This was all so wrong.

But my spear was gone and I needed another one. I swung my horse, galloped back, leaned over and yanked the spear from the hand of the man I had hurt. This spear was long, heavy, I shifted it, held it in my armpit, swung my horse again, went after another rider. By now, we were on the other side of the camp. The mounted men hadn't done too much damage; perhaps that wasn't the point. I couldn't think about that now. I tossed a third rider off his horse, and then a fourth. They were clumsy on their horses, unable to turn easily, their long spears getting in their own way.

But, by now, they had all had realized they were being attacked and finally, they focused on me. They pulled their horses around and charged at me. I pulled my horse sideways and around and we fled back through the tents. But by now the people had reorganized themselves, run for spears and knives. The horsemen met a line of screaming, yelling women and men. They swung their spears but spears are useless up close. They turned their horses again and fled.

I pulled my panting, sweating horse to a halt, slid off and ran, shouting for the tent, for Lani and the children. The children emerged, holding on to each other. But Lani was not with them.

By now, the people had also caught the men who had fallen. None of them were too badly hurt; the one I had speared in the back was bleeding hard but the spear had only torn a flap of flesh. The four of them were herded into the firelight, shoved to their knees. Kai lifted his head, stared at me. His white teeth flashed.

"They are men from Kazaan," I said, coming into the firelight myself.

“They are not men,” a woman shouted, “but wolves, trying to kill us all.”

By now the people who had been hurt were limping forward as well. One woman was bleeding from her head and another man was holding his side. And then Lani limped into the firelight; blood was soaking one side of her garment. She collapsed in front of us all.

“Look what you have done,” another woman screamed at them. “How could you do this? What is the matter with you people? How can you hurt other human beings?”

The men from Kazaan no longer looked powerful. They looked sick and frightened. They were very young men, really, even Kai. Perhaps they had thought it would all be a crazy adventure.

They put their heads down and didn’t look at anyone.

“What shall we do with them?” said Shuz at my side. People were crowding in around the men, screaming at them. One woman slammed one of the men in the head with her digging stick. He fell over and everyone laughed. Others began to swing at them also.

“Stop it,” I yelled, standing up from where I had been bending over Lani. I ran forward into the firelight. “Stop this. Leave them alone.”

But the people in the crowd were much like dogs that had scented a prey. They crowded closer. Some of our young men had spears in their hands. They poked and prodded at the kneeling men, not enough to hurt them, but enough to draw blood. The one who had fallen over was upright now and leaning on the shoulder of another man. The Kazaan men crowded closer together, huddled into one another to protect themselves.

Finally, I grabbed a spear and wrenched it out of someone’s hand and got in front of the kneeling men and turned to face the crowd.

"No," I yelled. "Let them go."

People had seen me on the horse, fighting. They fell silent.

"Let them go," I said again." Let them go back to their people and tell them about tonight. Let them go. They have lost. Let them tell their people to leave us alone, to stay away, so that there will be peace on the plains."

I nodded at the men and they stood up. Kai glared at me. He looked like a tiger ready to kill. Then the crowd parted. The other men grabbed him, and they passed through us, limping, leaning on each other, and went into the night.

"Go home," I called after them. "Leave us alone. Go home and live in peace. Be at peace. Tell your families. Come here no more."

The people crowded around. Someone built up the fire and sat there together. Everyone was talking, telling stories of what they had seen and done.

Shuz had gone inside the tent to tend to Lani, and also settle the children and soothe them to sleep. I went to check on Lani but she was lying very still with her eyes closed and Shuz was sitting by her. I went back outside the tent. People wanted me to tell the story of the fight but even thinking about it made me feel sick. Finally, after much talk, the people drifted away but of course, the camp still took a long time to settle. I could hear noise and talking and children crying from the other tents for a long time. I lay in my robes but I couldn't sleep.

And so I went and sat outside again by the fire, staring into its flames, seeing things pictured there, until the morning sun began to lighten the sky and the birds began to fly overhead. And then I fell asleep, sitting up, and I felt someone put a fur wrap over my shoulders but I didn't wake.

Chapter Eleven

"But we are safe now," I said. "They won't come back."

"No," Lani said. She was still under a layer of skins but Shuz had propped up her head on a folded robe. "I will never feel safe until we are far away from those people. Perhaps some of the other clans will come with us. A bigger group is better. Safer. "

"And go where? And do what? Wander some more through another strange land. Try to survive. Wear out our clothes and tents and freeze and starve through another winter. No. Come to the valley I found. We can stay there. Black Horse is near there. We could settle there."

"No," she said.

She tried to sit and then fell back. I stood and went outside. Outside, around us all the other clans, not ours, were packing with some speed. People were still upset and angry over the attack last night. When I went outside, most people didn't know how to treat me. They walked around me with their faces turned away.

Many people had spent most of the night talking. Some people wanted to stay and some wanted to leave and every clan seemed to have a different idea of where to go. Our clan wanted to follow the sun towards the mountains. We could see their white tips on the horizon. But no one in our clan would or could move until we knew if Lani would live or die.

As hurt as she was, she still had enough energy to argue. But she could hardly talk. The spear had gone into her back and now her breath bubbled in her throat. Shuz had gathered leaves and boiled herbs and made poultices. All the women came and went at various times during the day. The children were parceled out among the various tents. I came and went as well. I wasn't good at tending hurt people. I was impatient, angry and miserable.

I took the horses for water and grass and thought about going hunting but I couldn't go away from the camp. As soon as I tried to leave, a vision of Lani's face, peaceful in death, appeared in my head and I turned and ran back. She wasn't dead but sleeping restlessly, moving under the furs, muttering. Shuz tended her faithfully. There was nothing for me to do. Shuz looked up when I came in the tent, shook her head slightly at me for making too much noise. I left again.

Outside the tent, someone was waiting for me, a young man who seemed afraid to even look at me.

"Please come," he said. "She wishes to talk with you."

I had no idea what he was talking about, but I followed him.

We went to a very small, very tattered, ancient tent on the edge of the camp. The boy waved his hand at it and then left so I crawled inside. It was very dark and smoky inside; when my eyes adjusted, I saw a very old person sitting huddled in fur robes beside a fire that was only glowing coals. I sat down across the fire and waited. And waited.

Eventually he or she lifted her head and looked at me. It was a strange look. Her eyes were bright blue and seemed to see, not me, but somewhere just behind me. Her hair was twisted into long braids that fell to her waist. Her voice, when she spoke, was hoarse and croaking, as if she hardly used it.

"I am the shaman, Elin," she said. "Luz has told me of you."

I nodded.

"Do you dream?" she asked. "Can you fly in your dreams?"

"Yes," I said, "sometimes."

"Do you speak with the dead?"

I shifted my skinny bum on the grass. "Yes," I said.

Now her eyes were looking directly at me. "And can you speak with animals? Can you understand what they say?"

I wasn't sure how to answer this question. I liked animals, I had always liked them and sometimes I thought I understood them. Was that the same as speaking with them?

"Perhaps," I said.

She was silent for a long time. Then she said, "How did you learn to ride horses?"

"I just thought about it. I could see how it would work."

"And how did you learn to fight men?"

"I didn't learn. I was angry and afraid. I was afraid for my family and I had to defend them. But I don't want to fight again."

"Yes, of course. But what if you must? What then will you decide?"

She leaned forward and threw some dried grass on the coals. The smoke that billowed up was sweet and burned my already burning eyes. It rose in many colors and though there was no light, the smoke seemed to have light within it.

"You must learn," she said and frowned. "You will come to me in the next spring and I will teach you. There is so much for you to know. You must learn how to care for your people, how to guide them, how to interpret your dreams."

"How will I find you?"

She laughed. "How did you find this Gathering? How did you find the horses? How did you live when you were dying? You have more abilities than you think. You will come."

She said this with quiet satisfaction, and then she waved at me in dismissal. I stood up and ducked out through the low doorway and into the bright sun. I took deep breaths of air and then I went back through the camp to Lani's tent.

When I came inside and looked at Lani and at Shuz, sitting at her side, Shuz smiled. "I think she is better. She is breathing more easily and resting. But she will be weak for a long time, I think. She needs food, tea, herbs."

This time I went out of camp with Spotted Dog at my heels. I went to the highest hill and sat there while the wind blew in my ears. I thought about the old woman and her strange questions. Then I thought about the valley, about the river I had found, about the clear low pools full of fish, and how I had followed the river to the lake, the sandy beach I had walked on there, the long sloping hills of grass that surrounded the lake. I thought about the trees that could be cut down to make houses that would be warm when the winter winds blew. I thought about things my mother had told me, and the old woman in her black tent with the fire burning in colours.

I thought about the people of Kazaan and the young men who had come the night before, their faces when they charged into our camp, their faces when they left. I saw the anger in Kai's face when he looked at me. At the moment when I told him and his friends to leave, he wanted to kill me. That was the message in his eyes. I wouldn't forget, but neither would he. We would always be enemies. I had never had an enemy before. The very thought of it cut into my heart.

I thought about the many, many days that would have to pass before Lani would be fit to travel and the things that needed to be done before then. Tonight, I would stand before my people and tell them of their future and how it could be

And then I called Spotted Dog to me, and we went hunting.

Chapter Twelve

We called the new place Botai, after my mother. We settled on the shores of the lake, in the bowl-shaped valley, and we built houses out of logs and stones with hides on top, so they were both houses and tents. Some of our people found it hard to settle in one place and so they went on and continued to wander and then return. But the rest of us settled. We had traded for sheep and goats at the Gathering. We learned to spin wool, to weave cloth and we learned about new foods and a new way to live.

The horses became our closest friends and companions. One day the next spring, I watched a new foal suckle its mother. I went and found a clay bowl in my tent, came back and sat on the other side of the mare and squeezed out a bit of milk. I tasted it. Sweet, and if it made the foals grow, perhaps it would do the same for our children. From then on, every morning I went to the mares who had foals, and took several bowls of milk. We made the milk into all kinds of nourishing food. The horses now fed us, both meat and milk, carried us, helped us with herding the other animals.

Lani healed slowly, but she did heal. One morning, we sat together in the warm spring sun and looked out over our valley. Our houses and tents were on a flat area just above the lake. We had learned that the lake rose and fell with the seasons and built our houses where they would stay dry.

Below us, the horses grazed on new green grass. Birds tumbled and played in the sky and the wind licked the water of the deep blue lake. The wind brought the voices of children and the smell of smoke and cooking from people's fires.

Lani smiled at me. "I was wrong and you were right," she said. "You were wise, Morven, to bring us here and persuade us to settle. This is our home now. I wish your mother could have been with us here."

I shrugged. "Perhaps she is. I hear her voice sometimes on the wind or in the voices of birds. I feel her presence. I think she is near."

"And Dura?"

"I don't know. I don't hear him. I think he has gone on somewhere, perhaps on a journey."

"My son is so like him."

A group of children ran by, screaming and chasing one another.

"And you, Morven, will you ever have children, a family of your own?"

"No," I said. "I will not. I have other paths to walk, other plans. I have never wanted children. It is not for me."

We sat silent for a while longer. Then I said, "I am leaving soon. I am going to study with the shaman, Elin and then I will return. I will learn to travel in other worlds. Perhaps I will see my mother and Dura again. I think it will be frightening and wonderful. Even now, I sit by my fire at night and see things. But I know so little. When the spring is a little warmer, I will go. There is so much to learn."

"Be careful."

"Yes, I will."

Runners had come to Botai from other clans. There were always stories now, on the plains, of fighting. Sometimes I heard Kai's name mentioned by the runners. He was still angry. He was fighting the people of the plains. He stole horses and sheep and burned houses. But so far he had never come to Botai. Perhaps he would never come, but perhaps he would, and if he did, we had to be ready.

Our young men had learned to hunt with spears and bows from the backs of horses. Now many of them rode as if born on the back of a horse. We ate well these days. We ate fish and meat and milk and berries. During the last winter, there had been no hunger in the houses of Botai, no crying children at night. Babies were born fat and healthy. Life was good for all of us. Those of us who had settled never wanted to travel or fight again, and yet, we knew that the peace of our blue-green valley could be broken at any time. I watched, always, for a horseman on a hill, silhouettes against the sky, or the sound of distant hooves. I would never be caught unprepared again.

And now, reluctantly, I knew I would have to leave again. I put off the day of leaving. There was always a reason, a new foal to wait for, a new house to help build, a hunting trip to plan.

But as spring wore on, I began to think about getting ready. One night, I went to the men's fire and waited for permission to join them. Luz, the shaman, beckoned to me to come and sit. Someone brought me a bowl of fermented milk. The men and I were easier with each other these days. They still laughed and teased me when they saw me but in a respectful way.

"Red Crow," they would say. "What is the news from over the plain?"

I informed them that I would be leaving. "You must always be ready," I said. "Kai will never forget what was done. If he finds out where we live, he might come here. Listen to the dogs and the birds for warnings. Watch from the hills. I will return as soon as I can."

I desperately hoped I could leave Botai for a while, and all the people—especially Lani and Shuz and the children—would be here waiting for me on my return. I knew where my place was now. It was with my people. I had no questions about that anymore, but I had questions about many other things.

The next night, I dreamed myself into a bird and went flying over the plains, I flew over the flat plains; the grass was gold in the sun and blue in the shadows. Bright green trees lined the rivers and filled the deep ravines. I crossed the river far to the north and now I could see a brown cloud of dust. As I flew closer, I could see men and horses gathering beside the river. I couldn't see their faces, and when I tried to get closer a strong wind arose and blew me away. I awoke, surprised to find myself in my own sleeping robe.

That afternoon, the dogs began barking and running. I grabbed my bow and spear but it was a runner arriving in camp, panting heavily as he trotted down the hill. He was met by the children, who led him to Lani's tent. I followed them. The runner was sitting on the ground, shaking with exhaustion. He drank a bowl of fermented milk but his voice was shaky when he told us his message.

"More fighting," he said. "Many of our people were hurt. Kai and the others took some of the women and children." Tears rolled down his face.

I sat down beside the runner. "Tell us this story."

He told us of a sudden nighttime raid, of men on horses riding through their camp, of women and children grabbed and taken screaming. It had all happened so fast, he said. None of them had time to react. The next day, they had gone to the Kazaans and asked for their family members to be returned. The Kazaans drove them away.

"Kai has changed his name now. He calls himself Khan," said the runner. "I am going to all the clans I can find to warn them."

I put my face in my hands. How much of this was my fault? I was the one who had taught Kai about horses and lit this fire in him that would not let him be still no matter how many people he hurt.

"I will go with you," I said to him. "All the clans must make plans for how to fight him. You must learn to be ready. You must learn to guard your camp, to have horses and spears ready." The runner bowed his head in front of me.

I stood and left for my tent. What had I just promised?

The next morning, I finished packing. I tied my bow, my knife, a waterskin, and my sleeping robes into a bundle. I called Spotted Dog to my side and went outside to the horses. I was riding a new horse now, a horse the colour of the sun, with black stripes on his legs, like a tiger and a black mane and tail. I brought him to my tent, and slung the bundle on his back. Then I led him to Lani's tent. She and Shuz and the children came out and stood in front of me.

I looked at them all. "I am going now," I said. "I will return when I have done what I must do and when I have learned what I must learn. Stay safe. Take care of each other."

I looked at Lani and she looked at me. And then I slid onto the back of the gold horse and rode out of Botai. Spotted Dog, as always, was at the side of my horse. The runner went ahead of me to lead me to his people. I had offered him a horse but he preferred to run.

I stopped on the top of the hill to look back at the valley. It was hazed with dust and smoke. The sunlight struck through the haze so the whole of Botai seemed to be floating in a golden cloud. I knew then it would be safe until I returned.

The sun was warm on my shoulders and the wind lifted my hair. The golden horse shook his head and pawed the ground, eager to be going. I nudged his sides with my heel and we rode ahead into the blue distance.

ALSO FROM GREAT PLAINS TEEN FICTION

"The Fall *possesses an admirable grittiness.*" — Feature Review, *Quill & Quire*

When one teen dies in a tragic accident, the lives of three others are forever changed.

"utterly gorgeous!" — Tim Wynne-Jones, author of *Blink & Caution*

When no one listens, what's the point of talking?